FISH FINGERS
VS NUGGETS

JASON BERESFORD

ILLUSTRATED BY Vicky Barker

FISH FINGERS VS NUGGETS

JASON BERESFORD

ILLUSTRATED BY Vicky Barker

Catnip

CATNIP BOOKS
Published by Catnip Publishing Ltd
320 City Road
London
EC1V 2NZ

This edition first published 2018

3 5 7 9 10 8 6 4 2

A CIP catalogue record for this book is available from the British
Library.

ISBN 978-1-910611-04-3

Printed and bound by CPI Group (UK) Ltd, Croydon, CR0 4YY

www.catnippublishing.co.uk

To Cam, whose green orbs shall not dim
and whose legs are like a chicken's.

The only extraordinary thing about them was the extraordinary number of donuts Morris could eat without getting a tummy ache.

But then they met an elf.
And that elf turned them into
SECRET SUPERHEROES.

Now in times of trouble,
Gary Gamble becomes **THE CHIMP**, with the
springy agility of a chimpanzee.
Bel Singh, AKA **NIGHTINGALE**, flies and sings
with a voice so powerful it shakes the trees.
Ruby Rudd is **KANGARUBY**, who bounces like
a kangaroo and has a magic pocket.
And Morris Twiddle becomes **SLUG BOY** who
. . . er, shrinks to the size of a sausage and
wobbles about a bit.
They've vowed to help:

WHOEVER THEY CAN,
WHEREVER THEY CAN,
WHENEVER THEY CAN.

(Unless it's getting a bit late because they
might have to go home for their tea.)
Their superpowers only last for *an hour*
but when the four friends come to the
rescue they are totally fabulous.

In fact, they are . . .

ALIEN INVASION

Gary, Bel, Ruby and Morris were on their way home from school, and they were getting soaked. Raindrops pelted Fish Street like bullets and the wind howled like cannon fire. A silver streak flashed across the sky and they all thought it was lightning. It wasn't though.

'This rain is well rubbish,' said Gary from deep inside his green hoody. 'I wish I was The Chimp right now, cos I'd swing from a few lampposts and be home in like, ten seconds.'

'And if I was Nightingale I could fly over the clouds,' said Bel, shivering in her spotty waterproof. 'I wouldn't even get wet.'

Ruby was leaping in and out of the puddles. 'If I was KangaRuby I'd just dip my fingers in my pocket and pull out a pair of wellies.'

'Pair of wellies?' laughed Morris. 'Knowing that pocket, you'd pull out a pair of your gran's pants, followed by a trombone, a hedgehog and a soggy cucumber. None of them very useful in a storm.'

'I wish I had a soggy cucumber now,' said Ruby.

'Why?' asked Morris.

'So I could bash you over the head with it!' she said, laughing. The others did too.

It wasn't long before they arrived at Gary's front door. 'See you after tea,' he called as Morris, Bel and Ruby trudged off down the street.

In the clouds above, there was another flash of light as Zultar's flying saucer crackled with cosmic energy. Zultar was at the controls of a top-of-the-range VP20, with sunroof, satnav and under-seat heater. He did a loop the loop then flew low under Tumchester Bridge, skimming the ripples of the River Tum. Zultar was the best flying-saucer pilot on Planet Nrrmmff and he loved showing off. He swigged an iced coffee and boasted aloud, 'I am Zultar the Brave, Zultar the Warrior, Zultar the Magnificent!'

His satnav said, 'Ahead, keep right, you handsome hunk.' Zultar smiled. Everybody and every*thing* on Nrrmmff swooned over his good looks and he was sure the Earthlings would be dazzled by his gorgeousness too. This was unlikely, however, because Zultar looked like a chicken nugget. The only differences were his one tiny eye, his small mouth and his teeny-weeny tight trousers.

As Zultar performed more acrobatics over the town hall he began to laugh at his own brilliance.

'**Ha ha ha**, I am fabulous, I am amazing, I am . . .' Suddenly a real lightning bolt zapped the tail of the VP20, sending it into a dangerous spin.

'**. . . No! No! NO!**' he yelled, frantically jabbing the buttons on the flight deck. Lights flashed, sirens blared and the under-seat heater blew a fuse, setting his tiny trousers on fire.

'**Whaaaaaaaaaaaaaaaa!**' he screamed, dousing the flames with his iced coffee.

'Ahead, keep left, cutie pie,' said the satnav.

The flying saucer

screeched towards Earth, smoke billowing from its engine, sparks leaping from its tail. Zultar wrestled the joystick, but the ship kept on spinning, **DOWN**, **DOWN**, **DOWN**.

'Make a U-turn, you dishy devil,' suggested the satnav.

Zultar pulled and pushed the controls, jerked and jiggled the buttons, but it made no difference.

'**Whaaaaaaaaaaaaaaaa!**' he screamed again as the ground hurtled towards him. He gave the joystick one last, huge heave and . . . it was just enough.

'You have reached your destination . . . now show us your six-pack!' the satnav said, as the saucer sailed gently onto a traffic island in the High Street.

Zultar breathed deeply and wiped the sweat from his eyebrow. 'That was close,' he murmured, then unclipped his seat belt and headed to the door. As soon as he stepped outside though, the alien found he was surrounded.

'**You Earthlings won't take me alive!**' he yelled. 'I am Zultar the Magnificent!'

They all ignored him.

Zultar decided to fight his way out. 'Bow down before me or I'll blast you with my atomic liquidizer!' he shouted, pulling out a weapon that looked like a spoon, but still nobody moved. 'You've got five seconds!'

Zultar counted to five. 'Too scared to speak, eh?

Or just too rude? Well, you've had your chance, you fools!' He set his liquidizer to **DEATH (INSTANT)** and zapped his victims with 20,000 cosmic volts. After the blast, only smouldering, gooey blobs remained.

Zultar shrugged, saying, 'I did warn you,' then marched off up the High Street. The Nrrmmffian was feeling quite satisfied with what he'd done until he remembered he was under strict orders to keep a low profile. What was it the Great Elder had said? Oh yes. *Complete secrecy for the first three days.* Zultar thought he'd better stay out of trouble from now on.

A few minutes later, two road builders came back from their tea break and gasped at the traffic island in the middle of the High Street.

'Herman!' said one, shaking his head and pointing at the gooey mess on the grass. 'Have you ever seen anything so weird? Those traffic cones we put out have all melted!'

'Must have been struck by lightning,' said Herman. 'Unless they've been zapped by an alien!' The two men burst out laughing.

As Zultar walked through Tumchester, he soon realised there must be two types of Earthling: orange pointy ones (like those guys he'd just liquidized) and big, hairy ones that were much noisier. Luckily, none of the big hairy ones seemed to notice him as he picked his way through their legs. He walked past all sorts of shops and offices but didn't pay much attention until he saw some bright lights and a long queue snaking out of an open door. There was a sign in the window that read:

BIG MOMMA'S

Hole in your Tummy? Come to Mummy!

As he peered round the door, Zultar saw people wearing uniforms standing behind a counter. They had stars on their chests and Zultar thought, *Soldiers! I have found the Earthling Command Centre!*

A round woman wearing a feathery hat went up to the counter and one of the soldiers asked, 'Can I take your order?'

She is giving an order, thought Zultar. *She must be the leader – Big Momma. I will report this immediately.* He was about to return to the VP20 when something made him freeze. It was like a scene from a horror movie. Behind the counter, he'd spotted a laboratory where a soldier was holding a group of Nrrmmffians captive in a cage. They'd been stripped naked and Zultar watched as they were carried to a deep-fat fryer and lowered into a pan of boiling liquid. Zultar jammed his fist into his mouth to stop himself screaming. *Must stay calm! Need to keep out of sight. But oh, those poor souls!*

After a few seconds, the soldier lifted up the cage and Zultar could see the Nrrmmffians had turned a deep golden brown. Then they were tossed into a little red box. *Is that a coffin?* Zultar wondered. *Are they having a funeral?* The box was carried over to the counter and the woman with the feathery hat stepped forward and grabbed it.

What on Nrrmmff is Big Momma going to do with them? thought Zultar, but he didn't have to wait long to find out. The woman sat down, dipped the troops in something called B-B-Q Sauce and began biting their heads off! It was too much for Zultar. He pulled out his atomic liquidizer, set it to **BLAST (MASSIVE)** and pointed it at the counter. He pulled the trigger, there was a huge explosion and everybody ducked for cover. Zultar grabbed the only two Nrrmmffians who hadn't been chewed and hopped on board his atomic liquidizer. He set it to **GET OUT OF HERE (FAST)**, and rode it like a witch's broom back to his flying saucer.

'Murderers, torturers, kidnappers! Somebody is going to pay for this,' Zultar shouted as he carried the two Nrrmmffians into his spaceship and started giving them the kiss of life. He was surprised at how yummy they tasted but after ten minutes he gave up. 'They're gone but not forgotten!' he cried.

With tears rolling down his cheeks, Zultar switched on his computer and made a 4D hologram call to Planet Nrrmmff. The screen flickered and the Great Elder appeared, looking just like Zultar, except for a long grey beard and big bushy eyebrow.

'Hello, Zultar,' said the Great Elder.

'Hello, Mum,' said Zultar, choking back tears. 'I have terrible news. Some of our lads died tonight at the Earthling Command Centre. It's a place codenamed *Big Momma's* and . . .'

'Hold on. You haven't read the *Earth Guide*, have you?' asked the Great Elder.

'Er, no,' said Zultar.

'**ZULTAR!**' yelled his mum's hologram, grabbing Zultar by the ear and giving it a good tweak. (Nrrmmffian holograms could do this.) '**YOU NEED TO READ THE EARTH GUIDE!** I suggest you start with the section called "Food and Drink".'

'But what about our poor brave lads?' asked Zultar.

'They weren't Nrrmmffians, you numskull! Just

read the *Earth Guide*! Now, get to the hideout as quickly as possible.'

'Er, hideout?' asked Zultar.

'WE HAD A MEETING ABOUT IT BEFORE YOU LEFT!'

'Ah, *that* hideout. Yep. Got it. Sounds lovely. Just to be doubley-doubley sure though, can you remind me where it is again?'

'I built it in some rocks at the edge of Tumchester a thousand years ago,' said the Great Elder. 'It has everything you need to carry out your mission and save Planet Nrrmmff. There's also some milk in the fridge.'

'It's probably gone off by now,' said Zultar grumpily.

The Great Elder narrowed her eyebrow. 'Look, son, seven billion lives are at stake. We've nearly run out of energy and you're on Earth to steal what we need. The mission is too important for you to fail. Do you still have your Fact-Finding-Flies?'

Zultar checked his pocket. The three little robots were still there, red eyes glowing. 'Yes, of course.'

'I suggest you send one off as soon as possible.'

Zultar nodded and said, 'Right, lovely to talk to you, Mum. I'll start straight away.'

But the Great Elder hadn't finished. She scratched her beard thoughtfully then said, 'I know I told you this operation was in your hands, but I think you'll need some help after all. I'm going to send your brother down. Flunk may not be the brightest star in the galaxy but he's very good at . . .'

'Being an idiot,' muttered Zultar.

'*DOING WHAT I TELL HIM TO DO!*' said the Great Elder. 'Expect him shortly.' Then she hung up.

Oh no, thought Zultar. *The last thing on Nrrmmff I need is Flunk.*

UP UP AND AWAY

The Fish Fingers had agreed to meet at Gary's house after tea and Morris was the first to arrive. Gary's dad showed him upstairs.

'I hope you can get some sense out of him,' said Gary's dad. 'When he's playing with that hamster all I get are grunts.'

Morris walked into Gary's bedroom, where his friend was crouched over a hamster cage.

'Yo, brother,' said Gary sticking his hand out for 'knuckles'. The two boys had only just started greeting each other this way and Morris hadn't quite got the hang of it.

'**Yo**,' said Morris, missing Gary's knuckles completely and banging his fist on a cupboard door.

Gary smiled and picked his hamster out of the cage. 'He's a bit fat and goofy-looking, but cute, isn't he?'

'I guess so,' said Morris.

'I was talking to the hamster!' chuckled Gary.

'**LOL**,' said Morris shaking his head.

As Gary gave Morris the hamster to hold, there were more footsteps on the stairs and Bel and Ruby peered round the door.

'OOH, he's gorgeous!' said Ruby. 'Let me tickle his tummy, go on, go on.'

'Sure,' said Gary. 'I'll ask him. Morris, Ruby wants to tickle your tummy. It might be nice but I don't think she's washed her hands.'

'You're hilarious tonight,' said Morris, smiling at his friend. 'Just remember, *I'm* the funny one!'

'So which one am I?' asked Gary.

You're the brave one, the cool one, the brilliant at everything one, thought Morris. Instead he said, 'You're the ugly one!'

'OOH, that's fighting talk!' said Gary, so Morris quickly passed the hamster to Ruby and braced himself for the rugby tackle he knew would follow. It did. As the two boys rolled around giggling, giving each other wedgies, noogies and Chinese burns, the girls tut-tutted; at least Bel did. Ruby decided it looked like fun, so she handed the hamster to Bel and joined in.

Bel stroked Gary's pet under its chin. 'He's lovely,' she said. 'What are you calling him?'

'Ricky Junior,' said Gary, pinning Morris down with his knees and trying to fend off Ruby, who'd got him in a headlock.

'Like Ricky Zigzag?' asked Bel.

'That's **RIIIIGGHHT**,' said Gary from somewhere under Ruby's elbow.

'Cool!' said Bel. 'I absolutely love Ricky Zigzag.'

Ricky Zigzag was Tumchester's most famous athlete. He was a hurdler who'd broken dozens of world records and his face was currently on every billboard in the city because a huge sports event called the Trophy Games was being held in Tumchester in only ten days' time. The Fish Fingers had all got Ricky Zigzag posters on their walls, Ricky Zigzag pyjamas, slippers, socks, lunch boxes, pencil cases and sticking plasters. Morris even had a Ricky Zigzag sausage roll that he'd kept under his bed for the last month. (Pretty soon it would be growing arms and legs and running the hurdles on its own.)

Bel popped Gary's hamster back in its cage and watched as Ricky Junior jumped inside a little wheel and started scampering.

'**Hey, guys! Look at Ricky!**' she shouted. 'He's brilliant!'

'**OOh**, let's see!' said Ruby, letting Gary go. Gary wasn't expecting it so he shot forward, banging into a desk that knocked over a lamp, which sent a football-shaped piggy bank rolling along a shelf. As Gary walked away, Morris got up and the ball dropped onto his head with a crack. (Luckily, it contained only fresh air and dust because Gary never saved any of his pocket money.) Morris rubbed his head while the others gathered round Ricky Junior's cage, marvelling at the hamster's speed on the wheel.

'He's well fast,' said Gary. 'Just like the real Ricky Zigzag.'

'He goes like the clappers,' said Ruby, borrowing a phrase from her gran. None of the others had a clue what the clappers were but they guessed it was something that ran really fast. Or maybe clapped really fast.

'**SOOO** cute! I could watch him for–' Bel's words were interrupted by a loud **parp-parp-parping** from the street outside. 'Oh no. That sounds like Tereza's truck,' she said.

'Or a walrus practising the tuba,' suggested Morris hopefully.

'I thought we'd seen the back of her,' said Ruby.

'I wish we'd never seen the front of her,' said Morris.

The children started to feel the familiar tingle that happened whenever danger was nearby. Their superhero powers only kicked in if they were close enough to help and only lasted for an hour so there was never much time to hang around.

'Here we GOOOOOOOOOOOOOOO,' said Morris, whose body was wobbling and shrinking. He always seemed to be the one who transformed first.

Gary started to scratch under his arms, Bel began to flutter and Ruby found herself hopping up and down on the spot. Within seconds, the children had changed into The Chimp, Nightingale, KangaRuby and Slug Boy, with masks and pristine purple tracksuits to match.

Actually, three of them had tracksuits. Slug Boy was naked apart from his squelchy, sluggy skin and it was a feeling he'd never got used to.

'The Slug Mobile's in my backpack,' he shouted to Nightingale, and she fished out the clear plastic box that Morris now took everywhere. (Slug Boy was so slimy his friends usually dropped him when they tried to carry him very far.)

Nightingale popped Slug Boy into the Slug Mobile and hung it on her wrist. Then The Chimp somersaulted over to the window. 'Let's do it!' he shouted and the others followed him out. The Fabulous Four Fish Fingers landed nimbly on the pavement but the street was deserted.

'It MUST have been Tereza,' said KangaRuby.

'Well, she's scarpered. Again,' said Slug Boy.

'I'll take Slug Boy for a quick look around,' Nightingale said to the others, then she rocketed into the air with the Slug Mobile dangling from its chain.

'**SHHLLLLLLLLLLUURRRRRRRRRRRRDAAAAAAAAARRRRRRRRRRN**,' screamed Slug Boy, his cheeks flapping like socks on a windy washing line.

'What was that, Slug Boy?' Nightingale asked, soaring over the Fish Street School roof.

'**SLLLLLLLLLEEEEEEDOOOOOOOOOOOOOOOONN**,' said Slug Boy. He was trying to say 'slow down' but his lips were wibbling and wobbling so much his words all wibble-wobbled into one.

'Can't understand a word,' shouted Nightingale. 'Hang on, I'll slow down.' She jammed on her brakes above an electricity pylon. 'Now, what was it?'

'D-d-doesn't matter,' stuttered Slug Boy.

'Over there!' shouted Nightingale. 'Tereza's truck! I can see it!'

Tereza the Sneezer was a grotty supervillain who sneezed with the power of a hurricane and never used a hanky. For weeks she'd been stealing carrots to sell to eskimos as noses for their snowmen and she'd escaped from the Fish Fingers twice before. Her getaway truck was a dark green juggernaut on sixteen wheels that she called Thunderbird although everyone else called it Fnunderbride because

26

that's what was written on the side. (Tereza was a terrible speller.) Fnunderbride was now parked by a greengrocer's called Vince's Veg, its back doors wide open and ready to be filled with carrots. In the sky above, Slug Boy and Nightingale watched as Tereza strode up to the shop window wearing a belt with two holsters like a gunslinger, except instead of pistols she had twin pepper pots. She sprinkled a thick cloud of pepper into the air, sucked in a nose-full and **. . . SNEEZED!!!!!!**

It shattered the window, blasted the door off its hinges and left a hole in the brickwork big enough for a herd of giraffes in high heels to run through.

Nightingale and Slug Boy quickly did a U-turn and soared off to find the others.

ON A MISSION

The Nrrmmffian hideout was not far from Tumchester's biggest hill at a place called Wiggy's Bottom. Nobody knew who Wiggy was or why he had some rocks named after his bottom but he did. After throwing out the milk his mum had left (past its sell-by date by 999 years, eleven months and seventeen days), Zultar settled down to read the *Earth Guide*.

INTRODUCTION

There are many similarities between Earth and Planet Nrrmmff. Earthlings breathe air the same as we do, communicate in the same languages and live like us in many ways. However, since their technology is not as advanced as ours (by approximately 3,000 years) you will find some aspects of life on Earth confusing. This guide will explain everything.

Remembering what his mum had said, Zultar quickly turned to the section on Food and Drink. He'd eaten plenty of weird things on his travels – including a Mars bar made of real Martians – but he was still astonished by what he found in the guide.

FOOD AND DRINK

1. If you go into a coffee shop and see humans stirring their drinks with atomic liquidizers do not be alarmed. These are what Earthlings call 'spoons' and they are totally harmless. By the way, an Earthling will consider it strange if they see you stir coffee with your trousers. They do not have this custom on their planet.

... FOOD AND DRINK

2. Earthlings put something in their mouths called "chewing gum" but they never swallow it. Instead they spit it onto the floor as a gift for complete strangers. The stranger will stick it to the bottom of their shoe and wear it as a fashion accessory for the rest of the day.

ATTENTION PLEASE!!!!!

3. THIS IS THE MOST IMPORTANT POINT. DO NOT GO OUTSIDE YOUR SPACESHIP UNTIL YOU HAVE READ THIS BIT. I REPEAT. THIS IS REALLY REALLY IMPORTANT. I SHOULD HAVE MADE IT POINT 1 REALLY NOW THAT I THINK ABOUT IT...

'Okay, okay,' said Zultar under his breath. 'What is it? Don't tell me, Earthlings pick their noses and eat the bogeys? Who doesn't?'

... ATTENTION PLEASE!!!!!

Under no circumstances should you enter a cafe with a name like Chicken Lickin, Barry's Burgers or Big Momma's. These sell what is called 'fast food' and you may see something that will scare you witless. So be prepared. Take a look at *Picture A* below:

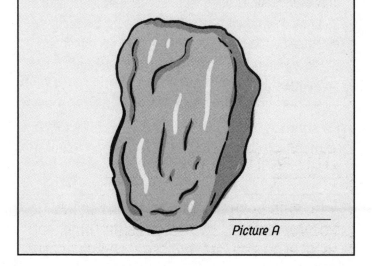

Picture A

'I've seen that face before,' murmured Zultar. 'Is it Crazy Dave who married my cousin Maureen? Looks like him, though it's a bit weird he isn't wearing any trousers. He might be on one of those nudist holidays. I suppose that's why they call him Crazy!'

... FOOD AND DRINK

Picture A is not Crazy Dave who married your cousin Maureen (although I admit there is a resemblance). It is what Earthlings call a 'chicken nugget'. <u>DO NOT MISTAKE IT FOR A NRRMMFFIAN ON A SECRET MISSION</u>. It is just a bite-sized chickeny snack, often eaten with barbecue sauce or tomato ketchup. No attempt should be made to rescue a chicken nugget. It does NOT need rescuing. To do so may blow your cover and jeopardize the entire mission.

'Whoopsy!' said Zultar. 'Probably should have read the Earth Guide after all.' He skipped to another section.

WHAT EARTHLINGS LOOK LIKE

1. Visitors often assume humans look like the cone-shaped, orange Dib Dabs of Planet Dig Dog because things that look like the cone-shaped orange Dib Dabs of Dig Dog are everywhere on Earth. But these are actually 'traffic cones' and they are used to

mark places in the road where repair work is being carried out. (Although nobody has ever seen any evidence of this repair work!) Traffic cones can also be found on the heads of statues for no apparent reason.

'**Ah, traffic cones!**' said Zultar. 'Well, the ones I liquidized this morning still deserved what they got. They were very rude.'

2. Real Earthlings (not traffic cones) come in all shapes and sizes but only a limited number of colours including black, brown and pink. Many of the pink ones glow like radioactive rizzoberries when left in the sun for too long.

3. Young Earthlings are smaller in size than adults but they are even noisier and have sillier haircuts. They wear uniforms to school and like to amuse their parents by coming home in at least one item that isn't theirs. Mums and dads then have to guess whose jumper, vest or trousers they are wearing. This game is called 'Whose Clothes Have You Got on Now You Dummy?' and is extremely popular on days when the young Earthlings do PE.

Humans are madder than a room full of Zonkian zoom turkeys with nits in their feathers! thought Zultar, skipping to another chapter.

CUSTOMS

1. Earthlings do not greet each other the way we do on Nrrmmff. If you lick your fingers and poke them in an Earthling's ears it will be considered weird. Most Earthlings prefer to shake hands, do high fives or kiss on the cheek. 'French' Earthlings actually kiss on BOTH cheeks so if there is a big crowd of French humans it can take many days or even years just to say hello. For this reason we advise <u>NOT</u> becoming friends with anyone French.

2. Earthlings often make a horrible gas in their trousers, which stinks like a dead Graarl worm. When they have made this smell, their custom is to point at somebody else and say, 'Was that you? It must have been. You're disguuuuusting.'

Utter, utter, utter nutters! thought Zultar, flipping through some more pages.

COMMUNICATION PART 1

1. Although Earthlings speak our language there are times when they make absolutely no sense at all. For example, if a teenage Earthling says something is 'WELL SICK' this does <u>NOT</u> mean it is 'HEALTHY VOMIT'. Our code breakers say it means 'very good'. When you are confused by what an Earthling says, just <u>smile and nod</u>. That's what they do.

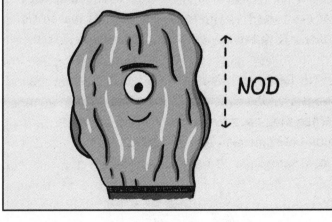

NOD

Zultar practised nodding and smiling. He soon got the hang of it.

COMMUNICATION PART 2

2. When Earthlings go to bed, they close their eyes and begin communicating in a strange language they call 'snoring' which sounds like a giant Zullooovian ningbat eating mud with its bottom. Our code breakers have not been able to figure out what Earthlings are saying when they 'snore' but we assume it is something silly.

Zultar waded through hundreds of pages until he got to the back of the book where there was a section called Useful Contacts. He discovered that Earth was full of crooks with superpowers who were happy to do nasty things to innocent people for selfish rewards and they were called 'supervillains'. Zultar glanced down the list of names that included baddies like Father Xxxmas, the Panteater, the Bog Snorkeler and Tereza the Sneezer.

'I don't think I'll bother with any of that lot,' said Zultar. 'This mission should be a doddle anyway. Earthlings are obviously all idiots and with any luck, I'll be home in a week and hailed as a hero. Then I shouldn't have to do another day's work in my life.'

HANKY PANKY

By the time the Fish Fingers reached Vince's Veg, Tereza was loading armfuls of carrots into the back of her giant truck and poor Vince was tied to the front bumper. He had a stick of celery in his ear and an aubergine stuffed in his mouth. The delicacy of his position meant the superheroes couldn't simply go charging into battle so they hid behind a postbox and tried to think of a plan.

After a lot of 'UMMMM-ING' and 'ERRRRR-ING' KangaRuby dipped her hand in her pocket trying to find some inspiration. She pulled out a bucket of live lobsters and a vacuum cleaner. 'Anybody got any ideas?' she said.

'Well, I don't know about the lobsters but you could pop me inside the vac,' said Slug Boy. 'Switch it to blow and fire me inside Tereza's big hooter. At least it would block her up for a bit.'

'Yes! Then the rest of us can rescue Vince!' said The Chimp. 'Genius!'

'Er, tiny problem,' said Nightingale, holding the

electric cable for the vac. 'We can't plug it in.'

'I'll knock on a door,' said KangaRuby. 'People are nice round here.'

She dashed over to the nearest house, carrying the vacuum cleaner in one hand and the bucket of live lobsters in the other. The woman who lived at the house, Mrs Hyde-Faddle, heard the knock and thought it must be a double-glazing salesman or somebody from the church. She never did business at the door so she put on a sour face before she even opened it.

'Hi,' said KangaRuby, 'sorry to bother you but I'm a superhero trying to defeat an evil supervillain who can demolish buildings just by sneezing and never uses a hanky and she's holding a greengrocer to ransom and stealing carrots, so I wonder, could I plug my vacuum cleaner into your electric socket?'

'What nonsense! Certainly not,' said Mrs Hyde-Faddle, trying to shut the door. But before she could do it, there was a thundering sneeze from the other end of the road. Tereza had spotted the Fish Fingers and she was firing a warning shot towards the postbox . . .

'AAAAAAAAAAA-CHOOOOOOOooo!'

The gust blew the postbox out of the ground and it took Nightingale, The Chimp and Slug Boy with it. It also shattered Mrs Hyde-Faddle's front windows and plastered the woman with blobs of snot.

'Are you *really* sure you can't help?' asked KangaRuby, still on the doorstep.

'Do come in,' said Mrs Hyde-Faddle, cleaning her glasses. 'Can I get you a cup of tea?'

Tereza's last sneeze had shaken the Fish Fingers but they were soon on their feet and a few seconds later KangaRuby was back with the vac all plugged into an extension cable.

'Right, I'll distract her,' said The Chimp, scrambling up a lamppost. 'You guys do the rest!'

While KangaRuby, Nightingale and Slug Boy ducked down a side street, The Chimp shouted over to Tereza. 'Hey, snot face! That conk of yours is big enough to have its own postcode! Stick a flag on the end and it could be a new country! You could call it *Nose-Ealand*!'

'**WhaAAAt?**' screamed Tereza. 'How dare you! My nose is **BEAUTIFUL!**' She grabbed both pepper pots from their holsters and sprinkled a great cloud of pepper into the air. Then she sucked in until her lungs were ready to burst and let out an enormous sneeze.

'**AAAAAAAAAAAAAAAAAAAAAAAAAAA CHOOOOOOOOOOOOoooooooo!!!!!**'

The sneeze carried cars, trees and hedgerows with it. It also sent The Chimp flying from the lamppost and spinning over the rooftops. 'That'll teach you!' Tereza sniggered, but the giant sneeze had worn her

40

out and she leant against her truck to rest.

KangaRuby spotted a chance, dashing out of the side street and firing Slug Boy out of the vacuum cleaner. He torpedoed through the air and shot inside Tereza's left nostril, hitting the back wall with a **THUNK**.

Slug Boy clung on as the villain coughed, spluttered and staggered backwards, desperately shoving her finger up her nose to try to get him out. Nightingale swooped into action. She dived for Tereza's leg and yanked off her shoe, then KangaRuby plunged Tereza's sweaty toes into the bucket of live lobsters.

'**YOWW!** That **HURTS!**' Tereza screamed, as the sea creatures snapped at her feet and snipped off her crusty toenails. She teetered on one leg and toppled to the floor.

Meanwhile, The Chimp was at Tereza's truck, untying poor Vince. As the shopkeeper ran off to phone the police, The Chimp opened the driver's door and was about to grab the keys, when he noticed a button that gave him an idea. He climbed nimbly onto the roof and shouted to the others, '**This way!**' while pointing to the doors at the back of the truck. The girls nodded, then The Chimp somersaulted off the roof and jumped into the driver's seat.

Tereza was still coughing and spluttering but she was starting to get her strength back. She kicked off the bucket of lobsters and blocked off one nostril with her finger. Then she blew with full force down the other.

'**Waaaaaaaaaa!**' screamed Slug Boy as he flew out like a bullet from a machine gun and landed in a puddle. While he lay spitting out water, Tereza

42

closed in on Nightingale and KangaRuby. She pulled both pepper pots from her holsters and dangled them in front of her nose, smirking. 'This is going to hurt you a lot more than it's going to hurt me,' she said. She spun both pots in her hands, tossed them into the air, caught them and gave them a massive shake. The girls held their breath. But Tereza found she was firing blanks; both pots were empty. The villain tried sneezing anyway but her puff had all run out. Angry, snorting, she charged head-down like a bull, towards Nightingale and KangaRuby as they stood at the back of the truck.

Tereza yelled '**GRRRRRRRRRRRR!**' but the girls were ready for her. At the last moment, KangaRuby bounced and Nightingale soared, and Tereza ran straight into *Fnunderbride*. As she wobbled, The Chimp pressed the button he'd found by the steering wheel and the truck tilted up like a see-saw. It sent a ton of stolen carrots crashing through the back doors, burying Tereza beneath them.

'I'm glad that's over,' said The Chimp, jumping out of the driver's seat.

'Too true,' added Nightingale. 'The greengrocers of Tumchester can sleep safely in their beds tonight.'

'I bet we've all got colds though,' said KangaRuby. 'Coughs and sneezes spread diseases, don't forget.'

'I'm starting to feel a sniffle already!' shouted Slug

Boy from the puddle. As Nightingale went over to pull him out, a siren droned in the distance.

'Best leg it before the police arrive,' The Chimp said, and the Fish Fingers ran off towards Fish Street.

A few minutes later, the police dragged Tereza out from the bottom of the carrot pile. She was groggy and wearing a very sorry expression on her face. The officers slapped her in handcuffs and quickly led her away as a red-eyed fly buzzed around her face. Tereza tried to give it a swat and thought nothing more about it. But the fly was the latest in Nrrmmffian technology and it had recorded everything it had seen.

A DYNAMIC DUO

The hideout was a lot bigger and better equipped than Zultar had expected. There was a hot tub, games room, home cinema and gymnasium, as well as a smart office where he could work out his plans. There was even a rocket-powered ejector seat for escaping in an emergency although, after reading the instructions, Zultar made a mental note never to go near it. (The manual explained: *Always always always wear a crash helmet. Danger of painful death or being grilled like a kebab during flight through Earth's atmosphere if you don't. This is not a toy.*)

Admittedly, the hideout was a bit too large for a Nrrmmffian but at least it meant the hot tub was the size of a swimming pool. Zultar stood on a desk in the control room and smiled as the Fact-Finding-Fly he'd sent to look around buzzed in and landed beside him. It carried the tiniest cameras, microphones and mini computers in the universe and it could even capture smells and tastes.

'Gotta love these Fact-Finding-Flies,' Zultar said

to himself. The fly's eyes flashed as it began to download its data straight into Zultar's brain. As the Nrrmmffian's mind filled with new information he slipped into a trance but he was suddenly woken by a ringing noise, followed by a loud knock.

Zultar shook his head and walked over to the door but before he could open it a giant ball of purple fur crashed into the room, bringing with it a cloud of dust and splinters. The fur had three legs, sabre teeth, one pointy ear and spikes on its back like a bed of nails.

'**Yoo–hooo, Zultar?** Are you home?' announced the giant.

CRASH!!!

46

There was a muffled cry from underneath the battered door, which the giant was now standing on.

'**Zulty!** Are you playing hide-and-seek?' asked the giant, who threw the door over his shoulder and found Zultar squished into the carpet. The giant grinned, licked his finger and poked it in Zultar's ear. '**Hiyaaa!** Mum sent me to help,' he said.

'Hello, Flunk,' muttered Zultar. He loved his brother, but Flunk had the strength of a brown bear and the brains of a brown shoe.

To be honest, there wasn't much of a family resemblance between Flunk and Zultar and there was a good reason for this. The Great Elder and her husband Mr Great Elder weren't Flunk's real mum and dad. There had been a mix-up at the inter-galactic hospital when Flunk was born but by the time the Great Elder realised, it was all a bit too late and she didn't want to make a scene.

'Come in and make yourself at home, I suppose,' said Zultar. 'Just don't break anything.' He looked at the door. 'Break anything *else.*'

'Thanks very much,' said Flunk. 'It's a lovely place you've got . . . oh, hang on.' He started bashing the desk with his fist. 'There's a nasty fly! Horrid little things, buzzing around spreading germs. Now, what were you saying, Zultee?'

Zultar gazed at the shattered remains of the Fact-

47

Finding-Fly and his desk that now looked like a box of broken biscuits. He took a very deep breath and closed his eyes. When he opened them again Flunk was still there, smiling helpfully.

'Did you remember the invisibility shield for your saucer?' asked Zultar.

'Sure did,' said Flunk. 'I put it on as soon as I parked. Mum gave me a bleeper and I bleeped it and when it bleeped the shield came on. I love bleepers. Bleepers are brilliant, aren't they?'

'Yes, bleepers are brilliant,' said Zultar. 'Look, go and have a rest. You've come a long way, you must be tired. I'll phone Mum and tell her you got here.'

'Righto, brother,' said Flunk. 'I'll go and explore the hideout.'

Zultar started sweeping up the shattered remains of his desk, the door and the Fact-Finding-Fly. He knew his brother meant well. He was just clumsy. Maybe they *could* work together. Maybe Flunk just needed the right guidance. As Zultar put the debris in the bin, Flunk shouted from the corridor. 'Hey, I've found a hot tub and a gym and a brilliant massage chair.'

'Yes, it's a great hideout!' Zultar replied.

'I'm going to give the chair a try,' said Flunk.

'Er, hang on,' said Zultar. 'What massage chair?'

'It's really comfy,' Flunk said, 'and it's got a big red

button and . . .' **WHOOOSHH!**

Flunk and the ejector seat hurtled at twenty-seven times the speed of sound through the roof, the clouds and beyond Earth's atmosphere into an orbit approximately 6,000 miles away. Fortunately, as it hit space, the seat's life-support system kicked in and wrapped Flunk up in a protective bubble. He now looked like he was swimming in a goldfish bowl, bobbing gently among the stars with his ear on fire.

Zultar could hear his brother's voice coming out of the intercom in the control room.

'**Zulty! Help!**' Flunk shouted. '**My ear hurts!**'

Zultar raised his eye to the ceiling (what was left of the ceiling) and took another deep breath. It wouldn't be hard to tow his brother back to Earth in a tractor beam but with Flunk around the mission was going to be much tougher. The whole plan needed a rethink. He would have to recruit some extra villains. Zultar remembered the list of 'Useful Contacts' at the back of the *Earth Guide* and went off to get it.

AT THE RACES

There was a huge buzz around Tumchester because the Trophy Games were just over a week away. TV crews were already arriving from all over the world, famous athletes were flying in and at Fish Street School every corridor and classroom was festooned with Ricky Zigzag pictures. All the kids were challenging each other to different events, like shoe throwing, puddle jumping, bogey flicking and longest uninterrupted whistle.

At break time Gary and Ruby were queuing for the water fountain when Snoddy and his lanky henchman Ferret lolloped over. Snoddy's hair was shaved into a little zigzag pattern at the side, just like Ricky Zigzag's.

'**Oi, Gary**,' snarled Ferret, whose teeth were sharp and spiky like tent pegs. 'Snoddy wants a race.'

'Yes, Gaz,' said Snoddy, 'it's that time of year for me to prove I'm faster than you all over again.'

Gary and Snoddy had been sporting rivals ever since they'd started school. They competed over anything and everything but most fiercely over running. Both were really speedy but Snoddy was usually just ahead.

'I can race you any time, anywhere,' said Gary. 'You don't scare me.'

'Yeah,' added Ruby. 'You're such a wuss, even I could beat you.'

'Ha ha ha,' said Snoddy. 'Girls are so funny.'

'What's that supposed to mean?' asked Ruby.

'Girls can't beat boys at running, it's a medical fact,' said Snoddy.

'He's right,' said Gary.

'Don't you go taking his side!' said Ruby. 'There's nothing medical about it. And someone who is fit and fast can beat someone who is out of shape and slow and it doesn't matter if they're a boy, a girl or a duck-billed platypus!'

'Whatever,' said Snoddy. 'Let's just get back to the real world. Gary, how about garden hopping, seven o'clock tonight?'

Garden hopping was a race across people's lawns, leaping over the walls, flowerbeds and fences in between. It was usually a winter sport because the dark evenings meant there was less chance of getting caught. Since it was summer, it was much riskier but that also made it more exciting.

'In Grimley Avenue,' Ferret said. 'Or are you too chicken?'

'Why Grimley Avenue?' asked Gary.

'The front gardens are big,' said Snoddy. 'So we'll be well away from the windows.'

'You're on,' said Gary. 'See you there at ten to seven.'

As Ferret and Snoddy wandered off, Bel and Morris came out of the school library. The others quickly filled them in on what had happened.

'I think you're walking into a trap,' said Bel.

'Snoddy is as slippery as a jellyfish in a soap-swallowing contest,' said Morris. 'And his partner in slime is worse. My advice is no, no, no, no, no and let me put it another way, **NO**.'

'You lot worry too much,' said Gary. 'I'm going to beat Snoddy and we'll be laughing about it for weeks.'

Under a tree on the school field, Snoddy and Ferret were chuckling. Grimley Avenue was where they both lived and the two bullies knew the gardens well. Snoddy and Ferret had been plotting this race for ages and codenamed it 'Operation Hot Dog'. They were going to make sure there was only one winner by fair means or foul. Preferably foul.

EYES DON'T BELIEVE IT

When Tereza the Sneezer woke up she was lying on a sheet of silky fabric that floated just a few centimetres off the floor. She was also staring into Zultar's one eye. It wasn't what she expected.

The last thing she remembered was doing sit-ups in the exercise yard at Tumchester Prison. It had been tricky because her hands were handcuffed, her feet were footcuffed and her nose was nosecuffed. Then there was a flash of blinding light and now . . . she wasn't quite sure.

Zultar assumed the dazed expression on his guest's face was because she'd never seen such a handsome hunk before. 'Can't quite believe what you're gazing at?' he asked.

'Er, yes,' Tereza replied. She decided it must be a dream but it was a very odd one because she seemed to be chatting to a chicken nugget.

'I took the liberty of removing all your cuffs and chains,' said Zultar.

Tereza paused then said, 'You're not from round

these parts, are you?'

'What makes you say that?' asked Zultar. 'Is it my trousers? We do wear them very tight where I come from. Or is it my accent?'

'No, not your trousers, no,' said Tereza. 'Or your accent really. It's just that you do have quite a resemblance to, er, a chicken nugget. Has anyone ever told you that before?'

'Can't say they have,' said Zultar, raising his one eyebrow.

Tereza smiled, got out of bed and made a dash for the exit.

'You're welcome to leave,' said Zultar. 'But I thought you might like to know why you're here before you go.'

Tereza had to admit she was curious. (She was also sure she'd wake up in a minute, probably in the prison hospital and everything would be back to normal.) Still, she decided to listen to what the nugget had to say.

'I'll start with the basics. I am Zultar the Magnificent from a distant planet called Nrrmmff,' he said. 'If you don't believe me, there's a large brick on the table. I suggest you drop it on your foot and if you're dreaming it won't hurt. If I am real, the pain will be real too.'

Tereza picked up the brick.

Zultar spent the next ten minutes rubbing ice on Tereza's battered toes. Then he carried on with the conversation. 'I'm recruiting a gang of supervillains. This planet has some things I need and my task will be much easier if I have a team of supervillains to help. If you decide to join me, you'll be handsomely rewarded.'

'What sort of reward?' asked Tereza, still nursing her foot.

'Whatever you like,' answered Zultar. 'Each member of the gang can draw up their own demands. In your case, I thought you might like to be paid in accessories for your truck – new wheels, turbo-charged engine, top-of-the-range stereo. With the addition of some Nrrmmffian technology I could even make it fly or dive underwater. By the way, *Fnunderbride* is parked in a cave in the basement. I towed it back from the police compound with a tractor beam.'

'*Fnunderbride?*' asked Tereza.

'Your truck. It's called *Fnunderbride*, isn't it? I saw it written on the side.'

'That spells *Thunderbird!*' scoffed Tereza. 'I wrote it myself! You Nrrmmffians might be advanced in technology but you're rubbish at spelling.'

'My mistake,' said Zultar, who knew it wasn't.

Tereza took in her surroundings. The walls were pure white marble. The lights above her head didn't have any wires, they just hovered in the air like hummingbirds and the strange silky bed was the most comfortable she'd ever slept on. It was all very remarkable. On top of that, if it hadn't been for the alien in tight trousers she'd still be in prison.

'Normally I work alone,' said Tereza. 'But maybe just this once I'll make an exception. Now, who else is in this gang?'

'My brother Flunk,' said Zultar. 'He's cooking tea for us so you can meet him later. But there's another supervillain. She's working out in the gym – I'll introduce you to her now.'

Zultar led Tereza to a lift that took them to a sleek corridor and he pushed through a door marked 'Viewing Galleries'. In the gymnasium below, a pimply teenager with bleached blond hair in a ponytail was sending a text. She wore basketball boots and a T-shirt with 'Wot U Looking At?' printed on it.

'She's called **Pizza Delivery Girl**,' said Zultar.

'Doesn't sound very supervillainy to me,' said Tereza. 'It's like being called Window Cleaner Woman or Shelf Stacker Boy. What does she do? Annoy people by turning up late, delivering the wrong pizza and not having the right change?'

'Just watch,' said Zultar.

Finishing her text, Pizza Delivery Girl spun, crouched low and pointed her fists at a target in the shape of a policeman. Two hot pizzas flew from her fingers like frisbees. The first chopped the policeman's head off, the second sliced through his legs.

'That's what she can do with thin and crispies,' said Zultar. 'But she can also make enormous deep pan pizzas. You could suffocate in one of those. And the toppings are despicable! Anything from minced camel phlegm to sliced scabs and the boiled hairs of an old man's toe.'

Suddenly Pizza Delivery Girl looked up at the faces in the gallery and squirted a jet of hot red liquid from her sleeve that sprayed across the window and dripped down the glass.

'Ugh, is that blood?' winced Tereza.

'That would be gross,' said Zultar. 'It's tomato sauce.'

'Does Pizza Delivery Girl have any weaknesses?' asked Tereza.

'A slight attitude problem,' Zultar admitted. 'She's only been here a couple of hours and I've had to redecorate her bedroom three times, she wants a 94-inch TV, she's addicted to sucking her own hair and is never on time.'

Zultar opened the window and shouted down. 'Looks like your workout is going well. There's somebody I'd like you to meet. Can you come to the control room in ten minutes?'

'You're like joking, right?' said Pizza Delivery Girl. 'I've got my nails to do, my nose to pierce and I've got nothing to wear.'

'Okay, get there when you can,' said Zultar, sliding the window shut. 'I just agree to everything,' he whispered to Tereza. 'It's the best way.'

A short time later, Zultar, Tereza and Pizza Delivery Girl were sitting in the control room drinking coffee and trying to make small talk. At least, Tereza and Zultar were trying to make small talk. Pizza Delivery Girl was texting on her phone.

'So why did your mum choose this place to build a hideout?' asked Tereza.

'It was by chance,' said Zultar. 'She got a map and just stuck a pin in Wiggy's Bottom.'

'Sounds painful,' laughed Tereza. 'I bet Wiggy couldn't sit down for a week!'

Zultar didn't really get jokes. 'I think you may be confused. Wiggy's Bottom isn't a person – it's a group of rocks,' he said.

'Yep, got it,' said Tereza, giving up on small talk.

There was an awkward silence until Zultar looked

at a clock on the wall and said, 'Guest number three should be here any minute.' He stepped towards a door marked WC and said, 'Don't be surprised by what you see. The last member of our team is quite remarkable.'

Zultar opened the door and Tereza found herself staring at a large white toilet. 'Very impressive,' she said, clapping her hands. 'Best disguise I've ever seen. Is it Chong the Changeling who morphs into any shape he likes?'

'Er, no, that's the lavatory,' said Zultar, staring into the toilet bowl. 'But our guest won't be long. I can hear him in the pipes.'

There was a gurgling noise and the sound of rushing water that grew louder and louder until it reached a crescendo and something slippery in a snorkel and scuba mask shot out of the toilet bowl before flopping onto the floor. He looked a bit like a mermaid but in reverse – with the legs of a man and the face of a fish. His eyes were big and bulgy and his teeth were far too large for his mouth. He also seemed to be holding a toasting fork, the kind you'd use for marshmallows.

'It's the **BOG SNORKELER**,' whispered Zultar, as the new guest began shaking off his drips like a shaggy dog. 'He's very powerful.'

'He's powerful smelling, I know that much,'

60

whispered Tereza, holding her nose. 'He stinks.'

Zultar gave her a (large) clothes peg for her (large) nose. He also put a peg on his own nose, saying under his breath, 'I'm told it's always wise to keep one of these in your pocket when you're in a small room with the Bog Snorkeler. He can be a bit whiffy. But he's amazing. He swims in and out of sewage pipes with ease and can pop up anywhere he likes – the toilet, the bath, even the kitchen sink – so he's a brilliant assassin. Oh, and you see that weapon he's holding, that's his trident. Ever since a nasty accident with an electric eel he's been alive with electricity, so if he points at you with that, **Kaboom!**'

The Bog Snorkeler took off his scuba mask. 'Greetingsss,' he said. 'Ssssorry if I'm little late, I lossst one of my flipperss in a U-bend near the Great Wall of China and had to go back for it.'

'Good to have you here,' said Zultar. 'I assume you're happy with the terms of our deal.'

The Bog Snorkeler nodded. 'Five million assorted sstickers of undersea creaturesss, delivered in a waterproof bag on completion of the misssion.'

'Perfect,' said Zultar. 'This is Tereza the Sneezer and the one over there texting is Pizza Delivery Girl.'

Pizza Delivery Girl looked up. 'What? Want a picture?' Then the smell hit her. '**Jeeeeeeez!** Has the new guy dropped one? It's like totally disgusting.

61

I'm going to barf!'

Zultar tried to apologise. 'Er, sorry, Bog Snorkeler. Pizza Delivery Girl can be a little rude at times, but she's young and we have to forgive her, eh?'

The Bog Snorkeler smiled and bowed low but it was clear he wasn't the forgiving type.

Zultar handed Pizza Delivery Girl a peg and they were all about to sit down when Flunk walked into the control room from the kitchen. '**OOH**, do we have visitors?' he asked.

'Hello, Flunk,' said Zultar. 'Everybody, this is my little brother. The last member of our team.'

'Great to meet you, guys!' said Flunk and he began licking his finger and poking it in everybody's ear. This didn't go down very well. Luckily, he didn't start stirring their coffees with his trousers.

After a few seconds, Flunk started sniffing the air like a bloodhound and his nose led him to the Bog Snorkeler. 'Excuse me, but you may have got some doggy doo doo on the bottom of your shoe,' said Flunk. 'Because there's a really stinky smell around here.'

As Zultar went to find another peg for Flunk's nose, his brother sat down next to Tereza.

'I'm very very very excited,' he admitted. 'I've never been on a proper mission before. I think there might be bleepers and everything. I've already got

62

one bleeper for my spaceship but I'm hoping there'll be more.'

'How lovely,' Tereza answered. Looking closely at Flunk for the first time, Tereza noticed he'd only got one ear and it looked like it had been barbecued. 'How did your ear get so burnt?' she asked.

'I went into space on a massage chair,' said Flunk, as if it explained everything.

Not surprisingly, Tereza was completely baffled but she smiled and asked, 'And why do you only have one ear? Is it an alien thing? Were you born like that?'

'No,' said Flunk. 'I lost the other when I tried to give myself a haircut with a chain saw.'

'Can't imagine why that turned out to be a bad idea,' said Tereza. 'Still, you learn a lesson like that once in a lifetime.'

'Yes you do,' said Flunk. 'And I even learned it twice in a lifetime because I cut another ear off when I tried to trim my beard with a chainsaw. I used to have three ears. They matched my legs.'

Tereza moved a bit further away.

When Zultar returned they all sat down around a table, except for Zultar who stood in the middle of it. 'Now, let me welcome you all properly,' he said. 'Never before has a team of such powerful supervillains been assembled. From now on we're a band of brothers and sisters and we must show no mercy in everything we do. We'll stop at nothing, we'll crush anyone who stands in our way etc., etc., etc. And I call on you all to raise your fists in a salute to evil!'

They all furiously punched the air except for Flunk, who didn't quite get it, and he waved his arms in a way that could best be described as 'jazz hands'.

'Before I explain the mission to you all,' said Zultar, 'we'll feast. My brother has just come from the kitchen where he's been heating up a seventeen-course meal.'

'**AH**,' said Flunk. 'I think there may have been a slight misunderstanding there. Because I was sure this morning you told me to "eat up a seventeen-course meal" which I have done very successfully. But now I'm starting to think you said "heat up" not "eat up" and . . . er, I think there could be a bag of crisps left.'

'**FORGET IT!**' yelled Zultar. 'I'll just tell them about the mission. Ladies and gentlemen, we're going to strike fear into the heart of Tumchester, steal a lot of furry little animals and save a planet.'

As Zultar went through the plot that the Great Elder had hatched, the supervillains around the table gasped. Even Flunk gasped and he knew it already.

65

RACE NIGHT

Gary and Morris walked up the garden path towards Ruby's front door at 36 Fish Street. Morris was wearing thick brown cords he'd grown out of and a purple jumper he hadn't grown into. Gary was wearing his cool green hoody, a running vest, shorts and silver trainers with Ricky Zigzag's trademarked zigzag flash. He knocked on the door and Ruby's pet parrot Marvin, began to squawk, 'MAAAARRRRVVIIIN'SSTTTAAAAAAAAAAAARVIIIN.'

'That bird's always hungry,' said Gary.

'He's a growing bird,' said Morris, who thought Marvin was a lot like himself. 'You need to eat a lot when you're young.'

'Marvin is thirty-six years old!' said Gary. 'Ruby told me.'

'It must be his hormones then,' said Morris, tucking into a jam donut he'd found in his back pocket. 'Or he might have big bones. You eat a lot when you've got big bones.'

Gary chuckled.

Ruby's front door opened and she bounded down the steps, pulling on her funky orange hat. From inside the house somewhere her gran shouted, 'Don't forget your cardigan!' but Ruby was already down the path.

'Gary,' Ruby said, 'you know we shouldn't be doing this, garden hopping is wrong on so many levels but I guess, if you really must, then we have to be there for you and it might stop Snoddy thinking he's the cat's pyjamas, the bee's knees or the frog's elbows or whatever it is.' By now she was standing at the gate and the boys had to sprint to catch her up.

At 33 Fish Street, Bel was sitting on the garden wall, reading a fashion magazine called *BFFL*. She looked like she'd stepped out of one of the pages. Her hairband, watch strap and socks were a matching purple and they were the perfect shade to complement her pale pink dress.

'Are you sure about this race?' Bel asked Gary as they set off. 'Because you can change your mind, you know.'

'I'll be fine,' said Gary. 'As long as Snoddy plays fair.'

The others shook their heads.

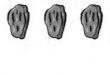

The sun was low when the Fish Fingers strolled into Grimley Avenue. Snoddy and Ferret were waiting on the corner. Snoddy was wearing black shorts and a matching T-shirt with a lizard's face on the front. Ferret had so much bling around his neck he jingle-jangled like a herd of reindeer. As the Fish Fingers walked up the road, Snoddy eyeballed Gary, and Gary eyeballed him back. They stared at each other like gunfighters, neither blinked, neither flinched and neither twitched as they approached. For Gary this was a big mistake because he was so busy staring at Snoddy that he banged into a lamppost and gave himself a nosebleed. Of course, it made Snoddy and Ferret cry with laughter.

'You won't find it funny in a minute,' said Gary, as Ruby dabbed his nose with a hanky. 'Because I'm still going to beat you in this race.'

'You're injured,' Snoddy said. 'It's obvious. The race is off and you can crown me the winner before you go. Just a small ceremony, no need for flags or the national anthem.'

Ruby stared into Snoddy's eyes and said, '**I'll race you instead**.'

'Hang on, Rubes,' said Gary, desperately trying to pinch the end of his nose. 'You can't take my place. It's too dangerous for a gir–'

'Were you going to say **"girl"**?? Too dangerous

for a **GIRL?** You *were* going to say that, weren't you?'

'Yes, no, sort of,' said Gary. 'But you said it was a bad idea in the first place!'

'I've changed my mind,' Ruby answered. 'I want to run.'

Bel took her friend to one side. 'But you've never won a single race at school, Ruby, even against other girls!'

'I've never *wanted* to win a race at school,' said Ruby. 'It always seemed so pointless. But this is different. I really want to beat Snoddy. *And* prove something to my friend Gary over there.' She walked calmly over to Snoddy. 'Are we racing or are you too scared of losing to a GIRL?'

'I ain't scared of nothing,' said Snoddy.

'So it looks like the race is on,' chipped in Morris. 'I happen to think girls can do anything boys can and if Ruby reckons she's got a chance I'll back her all the way.'

Gary's nose was still drip-drip-dripping. 'If you're sure,' he said to Ruby.

'I am,' said Ruby.

'Fine by me,' said Snoddy, taking off his tracksuit top and handing it to Ferret.

The race was due to take place between house numbers 4 and 76 because it was a long, straight stretch with fences and walls in between the gardens that were the perfect height. Morris volunteered to be the starter. Bel offered to stand on the finishing post to judge the winner and Snoddy said, 'I don't care where you stand. It ain't even going to be close.'

Ferret took up a position in the home straight opposite number 62 and Gary sat on the wall of number 10, still nursing his nose.

As the Tumchester church clock began to strike, the two racers went to stand together at the start line (the driveway of number 4). Then on the final **dong** Morris announced, 'On your marks . . . get set . . .
GO!'
Ruby and Snoddy dashed across the first lawn like greyhounds. Neck and neck, up to the first hurdle, a low wall. They rose together and landed level. Then they sprinted off across the next two gardens, jumping the flowerbeds in between, side by side. But Snoddy started to creep ahead. By the time they were at number 20, Snoddy was two steps in front and even managed to turn his head and flash a smirk at Ruby. It was just what Ruby needed. She found another gear, and little by little started to catch up. At the next hurdle, a thorn bush, she was still behind Snoddy, but by the next, a rickety fence, she was level again. Across the next three gardens, Ruby started to pull away. She'd found a natural rhythm

and although Snoddy was faster across the lawns he was a clumsy hurdler and it was Ruby who now opened up a good lead.

Approaching the home straight, Ruby was in front, muscles stretching, arms pumping, face relaxed, while Snoddy was tightening up, fists clenching, face snarling. Ferret didn't like it at all. Then he spotted something – someone – in the distance that made things a whole lot worse. Coming up from behind, a third competitor appeared to have joined the race: a grey-haired old woman wearing tartan slippers and carrying a cardigan. Ferret couldn't believe his eyes. It was Ruby's gran, leaping so high over the fences she seemed to have space hoppers on her feet and she was shouting, 'Put your cardie on, lovey, you'll catch your death of cold!' Her voice was barely a whisper though (since she was getting quite out of puff) and neither Snoddy nor Ruby realised she was there.

As the racers dashed across the driveway of number 60, Ferret could see that Snoddy was going to lose to a girl and not only that, the girl's grandma too. It was time to put 'Operation Hot Dog' into action and Ferret launched a pebble. He did it so sneakily nobody saw him but the stone soared high over a gate and hit the garage of number 62, clattering against the metal shutter. The sound woke a dog called Gruff who slept in a kennel outside and he barked like his tail had been jammed in a sandwich toaster.

'*GGGGGGRRRRRRRRRRAAAAAAAAAAAHHHHHH.*'

Of course Snoddy knew the bark was coming – Operation Hot Dog had been his idea, so he was ready for it. But Ruby was so startled by the noise she tripped over a garden gnome and fell into a flowerbed of daffodils, quickly followed by her gran, who tumbled in after her. Snoddy just laughed and skipped off towards the finishing line shouting, 'Champion! Champion!'

The other Fish Fingers rushed to help Ruby and her gran out of the flowers. Morris picked up the gnome, Bel pulled Ruby's gran up and Gary grabbed hold of Ruby's hand saying, 'You were well wicked! You'd have beaten him easy.'

Ruby's gran wrapped Ruby up in her cardigan. 'Tut tut tut, my girl,' she said. 'You shouldn't be running over people's gardens, especially without warm clothes on.'

Ruby still couldn't figure out where her gran had come from but as her head began to clear, the side door of the house opened and a man's voice shouted, 'Gruff, sit, boy. Good boy. And the rest of you wait there!'

Snoddy and Ferret were the first to react. They had no plans to hang around for a telling-off so they scarpered, running home like they'd been shot from a canon.

The others waited as the man opened the gates across his drive and came round to the front. They knew it was wrong to be in his garden and he'd got every right to be angry.

As the man stepped out of the shadows, Ruby stuttered, 'I'm so, so sorry,' tears welling up in her eyes. 'I'll pay for any damage.'

'If   that

gnome's broken, you will, kiddo,' said the man. Ruby looked up for the first time and found she was staring into the warm, dark eyes and glittery gold tooth of . . . no. It couldn't be, could it? Ruby tried to speak but her mouth had stopped working. Everybody's had.

'Did you hear me, kiddo?' said the man.

'A-a-absolutely, no problem, d-d-definitely,' spluttered Ruby. Then she asked, 'Are you . . .

Ricky Zigzag?'

The man's tone suddenly changed. 'Er, people do make that mistake sometimes,' he said 'But I'm er … a lookalike! Yes, that's it. A lookalike. I turn up at parties and shake hands, pose for photos, you know. Right, good to see you and from now on, keep off the grass.' The man turned to go but just then a phone in his pocket rang and he took it out. 'Ricky Zigzag here,' he answered, then stopped, realising he'd given the game away.

The children made big **O**s with their mouths and started dancing on the spot with giddy excitement. Even Ruby's gran was bouncing up and down, pointing at the superstar. Ricky spoke into his phone again, 'Look, I'll call you back. Something's come up.' He looked at the four beaming children and the elderly lady jumping around in her fluffy slippers and decided to trust them all. 'Yes, I'm Ricky Zigzag,' he admitted.

'*The* Ricky Zigzag?' said Ruby. 'The one on the telly and in the papers and magazines and posters and Blimey O'Riley!'

'Yes, I am all of the above,' he said. 'Except Blimey O'Riley. I'm not sure who he is!'

'We've all got your pencil cases and rubbers and lunch boxes,' said Bel.

'I even named my hamster after you,' said Gary.

'And I've got one of your sausage rolls,' added Morris. 'It's under my bed.'

'Er, great,' said Ricky.

'But aren't you supposed to be in a secret training base in the Peruvian mountains or something?' asked Bel.

'That's what I told reporters,' said Ricky. 'But I'm staying here at my cousin's house until the Trophy Games begin. I look after his dog and it keeps the media off my back, so you must promise you won't tell anyone.' He winked.

'Jumping jellybeans!' said Ruby. 'Don't worry, your secret's safe with us! Promise!'

'Well, I'm delighted to meet you,' laughed Ricky.
Then he looked at Ruby's gran and asked, 'Er, aren't
you a bit old to be garden hopping?'

'I was just bringing Ruby's cardie,' she answered.

'Hey, how do you know it's called garden
hopping?' asked Gary.

'That's what we called it when I was growing up
round here,' said Ricky. 'And I'll tell you another
secret. It's how I learned to hurdle in the first place!'

WHO LET THE HAMSTERS OUT?

Meanwhile at Wiggy's Bottom, Zultar and his gang were getting ready for the first part of their mission. Their target was a shop on the outskirts of Tumchester called Friends Fur-ever which specialised in small pets. Tereza, Pizza Delivery Girl, Flunk and the Bog Snorkeler piled into *Fnunderbride* and Zultar rode ahead, towing the truck in a tractor beam. It meant they didn't get stuck in any traffic jams and at top speed the atomic liquidizer flew so fast it was invisible to the naked eye (to be honest, it would have been invisible to a fully clothed eye too). They arrived at the pet shop in seconds and Zultar joined the others in the back.

'Just to be clear, it's only hamsters we are after right?' said Tereza.

'Of course,' said Zultar.

'But I still don't know *why* we're doing it,' Tereza said. 'Was I powdering my nose when you told everybody?'

'All will be explained,' said Zultar. 'For now, let's

11

focus on nabbing the little creatures.' He got out a map and went through the plan. 'We need to make our attacks here, here and here. But be careful. The owners live above the shop and we want to keep surprise on our side.'

The others did a thumbs-up, then they all stepped slowly out of the truck and hid in the shadows by the side of the building.

'No talking from now on,' whispered Zultar.

'None at all' agreed Flunk. 'Because we need to catch them unawares. So talking is a no-no-no.'

Everybody nodded.

'And that includes no chatting, whistling or telling jokes,' said Flunk. 'Not even a funny joke like, Why is a Zulloovian wasp like a banana? Because he's got onions in his socks! **HA HA HA!** Heard it before, eh? Anyway, like I said, no singing, shouting or yodelling. No playing the banjo. All these are forbidd–'

'Stop talking' hissed Zultar.

'I agree,' said Flunk. 'And when I say stop talking, I mean zero, none –'

'**WILL YOU SHUT UP!**' hissed Tereza.

A light came on in an upstairs window.

'Look what you've done now, sssilly,' said the Bog Snorkeler.

'It wasn't me!' said Flunk. 'It was somebody else who has quite a large nose but I'm not saying who.

Because I'm not the type to go telling t–'

Zultar pointed his atomic liquidizer at his brother and gave him a very hard, one-eyed stare. Flunk put his finger on his lips.

Lying in bed upstairs at Friends Fur-ever, Tracy Blewitt nudged her husband to wake up. 'Baz, I think I heard something.' Barry was snoring so Tracy nudged him again. 'Have a look, love.'

Grumpily, Barry peeked through the curtains. He couldn't see anything. 'Probably just the wind,' he said. 'But now I'm up, I'm going to sit on the throne. Last night's chicken curry didn't agree with me.'

Outside in the shadows, the Bog Snorkeler pulled up a drain cover and dived into the pipes below. Pizza Delivery Girl skulked by the front door while Zultar, Flunk and Tereza darted round to the rear. Zultar set his atomic liquidizer to **_HOLOGRAM (CUTE)_** and projected an adorable kitten at the back door.

By now sitting comfortably, Barry was reading a copy of his favourite magazine, *Gerbils With Hats On*. He heard the cat's meow and shouted to his wife to investigate. Tracy slipped into her dressing gown and crept downstairs. She peered through the curtains and shone her torch though the window. In the gloom she picked out the shape of a cute little kitty and Tracy breathed a sigh of relief. She guessed it must be one from the shop.

'Poor little mite,' she said. 'How on earth did you get out there?'

Meanwhile, the Bog Snorkeler was swimming up the sewage pipes and round the U-bend towards Barry Blewitt's lavatory. Soon the supervillain saw a light at the end of the tunnel and he grinned like a shark when it spots a seal bobbing in the water. Barry turned another page of his magazine, chuckling at a picture of a gerbil in a pretty tiara. Target identified, the Bog Snorkeler pointed his trident at Barry's buttocks and blasted them with so many volts it could've sent the poor man to Mars. As it was, Barry flew only as far as the bathroom ceiling where he banged his head on a light and knocked himself out.

Downstairs, Tracy was turning off the shop's a l a r m and

unlocking the back door. She was about to pick up the kitten when Tereza the Sneezer unleashed a gust of wind that knocked the shopkeeper off her feet and splattered her in so much snot she stuck to the wall. Tracy didn't even have time to scream.

With both Mr and Mrs Blewitt taken care of, it didn't take Zultar's gang long to find the hamster cages and start loading them onto Tereza's truck.

'This is, like, so easy,' said Pizza Delivery Girl, as she lifted two more cages into the back.

'Sssssimple,' smirked the Bog Snorkeler.

'Like stealing maggot cake from a Xanabian trouser fish,' said Zultar.

Flunk found he could pick up six cages at a time, but he soon got distracted because he was hungry. It seemed like hours since his last meal (this was true, although his last meal had been seventeen courses long) but his appetite was now running away with itself. Flunk spotted a display of dog chews in the

corner of the pet shop, gave one a little lick and then swallowed it whole. 'Hey, these are pretty good! You should try them,' he shouted to the others.

Not surprisingly, nobody else fancied a nibble but it didn't put Flunk off. After eating the entire dog-chew display (including the stand), Flunk helped himself to birdseed, goldfish flakes, guinea pig pellets and chocolate for cats. 'It's like a five-star restaurant in here!' he yelled.

Despite Flunk spending more time eating than carrying, it wasn't long before the crooks were ready to leave. But as they were heading for the door they heard a voice on a loud hailer. Tracy Blewitt had wriggled free and called 999 so now a police car with two officers was parked outside.

'We're the police,' shouted an officer called Alfie. 'Come out with your hands up.'

'And don't do anything funny,' his partner Janice added.

'I guess I can't tell them my Zulloovian wasp joke then?' whispered Flunk.

Pizza Delivery Girl was the first of the gang to step outside. She walked through the pet shop door with her hands in the air and Alfie stepped forward to arrest her. But the supervillain swiftly brought her hands down, launching two deadly thin and crispies.

The first pizza (made with fish eyes and belly-button fluff) sliced through Alfie's loudhailer and lodged itself so far into his mouth the police tug-of-war team would need to pull it out. The second pizza (toilet brush and armpit sweat) sliced through Janice's helmet, taking the top off her hair and leaving her styled like a Franciscan monk.

'Oi!' she yelled. 'My hair is police property! Not to mention *my* property. You'll get ten years for this.'

'And I'm like sooo scared,' sniggered Pizza Delivery Girl.

Janice picked up her hat (and her hair) and aimed her police pistol. 'Right, that's it,' she shouted. 'You're not going to make me look ridiculous.'

'Want to bet?' sniggered Zultar, stepping out of the shadows. He set his atomic liquidizer to **DANCE (IN YOUR PANTS)** and pulled the trigger, blasting both police officers at once. Seconds later, Alfie and Janice were stark naked except for their undies and boogying the Macarena by the side of the road. Janice was wearing Incredible Hulk pants but Alfie was wearing a pair of his grandma's enormous bloomers.

Zultar and his gang quickly made their escape and were soon back at the hideout. Once the hamsters had been unloaded, they all assembled in the control room.

'Congratulations,' said Zultar. 'You've done well. Our first raid was a resounding success. By the end of the week, there shouldn't be a hamster left in Tumchester.'

'So now are you going to tell us exactly why we're doing it?' said Tereza. 'I thought your planet was running out of power. What's that got to do with stealing hamsters?'

'Sshouldn't we be sstealing a nuclear power sstation or ssomething?' asked The Bog Snorkeler.

'Or like batteries from phones and stuff?' added Pizza Delivery Girl.

'No, no,' said Zultar. 'Too much toxic waste in nuclear. And batteries run out.'

'What about a windmill then?' asked Tereza, who felt that her nose made her an expert on gusts of wind.

Zultar shook his head. 'Let me explain. On Nrrmmff, hamsters give us our energy. They run on their little wheels all day, which we rig up to our power plants. Hamsters are eco-friendly, reliable and quite cute. But a terrible disease has drastically destroyed our hamster population and now we need to replace them. Fast.'

'Couldn't you just like, buy some?' asked Pizza Delivery Girl.

'It's a lot quicker to steal what we need,' said Zultar. 'And besides, we Nrrmmffians are a nasty, war-like people. We rob, cheat and lie. It's what we do.' He looked at the assembled crooks around the table and shouted, 'I'm sure you understand that.'

The gang went off to their quarters and as Zultar settled into his bunk he decided to end his very successful evening with a few laughs by flicking through the *Earth Guide* again. He opened it at random and – as usual – couldn't believe how silly the Earthlings were.

SPORT

Earthlings love nothing more than to argue and they have turned this into a sport they call 'Football'. Two teams compete to shout at a man called 'the referee' whilst kicking a ball around a field. When the referee blows his whistle, the players gather round him and shout and if a player shouts really well he is shown a yellow card. If a player does it really, really, really well he is shown a red card and then he can leave the pitch and sit down with his friends.

BIRTHDAYS

Earthling children are always getting coughs, colds and diseases, which give them spots and make their noses run. Earthling parents don't try to stop these illnesses spreading, however. Instead they throw a big party once a year called a 'Birthday Party' to share the germs around. After a song, a cake is brought out with candles on top and the 'Birthday Boy' or 'Birthday Girl' takes a deep breath before showering the cake with spit, snot and tongue dribble. The cake is then divided up amongst all the party guests who take the diseases home with them.

Very soon, Zultar laughed himself to sleep.

TV TIMES

At school the next day, Snoddy and Ferret spotted the Fish Fingers in the school canteen and soon slithered over, like rattlesnakes with something nasty to shake about.

'Hello, losers,' said Snoddy. 'What's it feel like to eat humble pie?'

'It's chicken and mushroom actually,' said Morris pointing to his lunch. 'And it's not bad although I think they've over-salted the chicken a little.'

'The only chicken around here is you, Doris,' said Ferret. Then he spotted what Morris was wearing on his feet (inside his shoes). It was a pair of Sick Socks, which were probably the least fashionable item of clothing ever invented. They made verruca socks look cool. The TV adverts said, *If your little cherub needs to throw up and he's miles from a bucket, help is at hand. Or rather, at foot! Children can simply take off a Sick Sock and chuck up into it. So, before you take them to the doc's, put them in our socks!'*

Sick Socks were made from a hi-visibility,

waterproof material and they had a zip round the ankle so they could be emptied out later. They'd been invented by a man from Tumchester and the idea had put Tumchester on the map. (Admittedly, it was a small map. Just a map of Tumchester really but it had made the inventor a fortune.) Morris hated his Sick Socks ever since he threw up into one and then absent-mindedly put his foot back inside before emptying it. But Morris's mum made him wear a pair every time he looked pale.

'I can't believe you've got those dorky socks on again!' said Ferret. 'Just when I thought you couldn't get any more dorky, you out-dorkify yourself!'

Morris mumbled something about Sick Socks being very hygienic but he knew he was beaten and he concentrated on finishing his lunch.

Snoddy turned his attention to Ruby. 'Tripped over any garden gnomes lately?' he asked.

'Not today, no,' answered Ruby.

'Such a shame you lost that race. Still, at least your gran was there to dry your tears,' said Snoddy.

The muscles in Gary's stomach knotted. 'Ruby only lost because she fell over,' he said.

'Yeah, she got a bit scaredy-waredy because that big doggy did a woof woof,' said Snoddy.

'No,' said Gary. 'And anyway, I'm glad she tripped over because if she hadn't, we wouldn't have met

Ricky Zigzag.'

Bel, Ruby and Morris looked sideways at Gary.

'You never met Ricky Zigzag!' said Snoddy. 'You're lying.'

'Ha ha, yes he is,' said Morris. 'Well, not lying, just joking. We also met Spider Man, Cinderella and the President of Belgium, didn't we guys? Ha ha ha.'

'Funny,' said Snoddy. 'And I mean funny weird not funny hilarious.'

The bullies sidled off as Morris, Ruby and Bel all turned to Gary.

'What did you say that for?' asked Bel sternly.

'Ricky is supposed to be top secret!' said Ruby.

'We promised him, mate,' said Morris. 'We can't go blabbing to anyone.'

'Snoddy just winds me up,' answered Gary.

'He winds us all up,' said Ruby.

89

After school, the Fish Fingers went to Ruby's house for a bounce on her trampoline. They were all leaping around when they overheard the headlines for *Tumchester Tonight* coming from the living room. 'Good evening,' said the host, Dickie Trickle, 'but it wasn't a good evening for the owners of Friends Fur-ever who were attacked by a gang of supervillains last night.' The children rushed inside to find out what had happened.

Dickie Trickle was a man with shiny teeth and shiny ties who wore glasses as big as TV screens. 'The bad guys barbecued Mr Blewitt's buttocks and battered Mrs Blewitt with bogies,' he carried on.

'Bogies? Sounds like Tereza,' said Bel.

'We're joined now by the man in charge of the case, Detective Rigley, who's well known to our viewers,' said Dickie Trickle. The camera panned to a policeman with a bald head and a moustache that looked like a black caterpillar asleep under his nose. 'So, Detective, what can you tell us about the raid?'

'It was most disturbing,' said Rigley. 'No money was taken and only one kind of animal. Our evidence suggests the crooks were stealing hamsters.'

'Hamsters?' said Dickie. 'Despicable!'

'I think they're quite cute myself,' said Rigley. 'Especially when they run around on their little wheels.'

'*Stealing* hamsters is despicable,' said Dickie.

'Good point,' nodded Rigley. 'We did have two officers at the scene and I can now show you some shocking CCTV footage.'

The picture cut to Alfie and Janice being attacked by Pizza Delivery Girl's flying missiles.

'The supervillain in this footage is the infamous Pizza Delivery Girl,' said Rigley. 'She might sound nice. Everyone likes pizza and everyone likes girls, but she's rotten to the crust.'

The CCTV pictures then showed Alfie and Janice dancing in their pants.

'The male officer seems to be wearing a giant pair of ladies' undies,' said Dickie.

'That is correct,' said Rigley. 'But I'm told it was a one-off, caused by a faulty washing machine and the fact that his auntie Beryl was staying for a week. The broken washing machine caused a backlog in the laundry basket and as a result there were no other clean pants in the house that day.'

'Sounds reasonable,' said Dickie. 'Let's move on to the rest of the film.'

In the next bit of CCTV footage the crooks were carrying hamster cages to Tereza's truck.

'We've identified two of the villains as the notorious Tereza the Sneezer and the lavatorious Bog Snorkeler,' said Rigley. 'Tereza vanished from Tumchester Prison just a few days ago and that's her truck they're using. The Bog Snorkeler hasn't been seen in these parts for a while so to help the public identify him we've produced these scratch and sniff Wanted posters.' Rigley took one from his pocket and handed it to Dickie, who rubbed it with his finger and held it up to his nose. Immediately he fell off his stool. From somewhere under the desk Dickie spluttered like a cat coughing up a fur ball.

'TH-THAT'S DIS . . . GUS . . . TIIIING,' he gasped.

Rigley carried on speaking, even though all he could see now was the top of Dickie's head.

'The next two crooks are something of a mystery,' he said. The picture froze and zoomed in on what appeared to be a chicken nugget holding a spoon. 'We believe this is the ringleader.'

Dickie clambered back on his chair. 'Are you sure that's not somebody's lunch?'

'It could be,' said Rigley. 'But if it is, why's it wearing tight trousers and carrying a spoon? No, we believe it's the brains of the operation.' The picture then zoomed in on Flunk. 'And we believe this is the thicko of the operation. He was spotted eating dog chews and birdseed at the pet shop. But just like the nugget, he hasn't shown up anywhere on our police computers. We suspect they're both foreigners. Interpol are checking their databases as we speak.'

'You don't seem to have many leads,' said Dickie.

'I can't deny it,' said Rigley. 'The crooks appear to have vanished. We have no clues, no fingerprints and no idea where they are. In short, the police have nothing to go on. And neither does Barry Blewitt after what the Bog Snorkeler did to his toilet.'

'Is that it?' asked an exasperated Dickie.

'I do have one piece of important information,' said the policeman. 'We've come up with a great nickname for the gang: The Nuggets.'

'But they don't all look like chicken nuggets,' said Dickie. 'Just one of them.'

'True, but to mention all the crooks in one big nickname you'd end up with something like **The Sneezy–Stinky–Monstery–Pizzary–Nuggety–Gang.** Far too complicated. So we're sticking with **The Nuggets.**'

'Thank you, Detective,' said Dickie, turning to another camera. 'Now sport and the build-up to the Trophy Games continues with –'

'Er, do you need me for this bit?' interrupted Rigley. 'I know I'm not an athlete but I did come third in the police pancake race this year and would have come second if a passing squirrel hadn't stolen my pancake.'

'No, we don't need you for this bit,' said Dickie.

'Do you need the squirrel?' said the policeman. 'I know where he lives.'

'Also a no,' said Dickie.

LOOK OUT PET

The Fish Fingers all went to bed early but they wore dark clothes under their pyjamas. One by one, when their parents were downstairs watching TV, they sneaked out of their bedroom windows and assembled by the gates of Fish Street School. With no way of knowing which pet shop to stake out, the Fish Fingers chose the biggest in Tumchester, a two-storey superstore called Paws and Claws. It also happened to be the place where Gary and his dad had bought Ricky Junior.

The children huddled in an old red telephone box outside Paws and Claws trying to figure out their next move.

'If they do come,' said Morris, 'we'll be outnumbered, so we need to outsmart them. We've never fought this many supervillains before and it'll be the biggest test of our lives. We need a proper plan.'

There was a long silence as the Fish Fingers tried to think and then Ruby said, 'I've got it. How about we jump out of a bush?'

'Jump out of a bush?' said Morris. 'We're fighting five of the nastiest supervillains in the universe who'll be attacking us with horns, razor-sharp pizza, electric tridents, magic spoons and a hurricane of snot, and our plan is . . . jump out of a bush? I'm not sure it'll be quite enough!'

'Okay,' said Bel, 'how about two of us jump out of a bush and the other two find a way into the shop? '

'It's fifty per cent better than all of us jumping out of a bush but it's still a plan that relies heavily on *jumping out of a bush*!' said Morris. 'And we're not really spoiled for choice in the bush department.' Morris pointed to the only bush within 200 yards. It wasn't very big. More of a shrub. And there was a melted ice lolly underneath it, crawling with ants. 'I'm not jumping out of that bush.'

'We could jump out of a bin then?' said Ruby.

'Fine, a bush it is!' said Morris, grumping off to hide.

'Don't worry,' Ruby said to the others. 'I'll keep him company.'

As swiftly as they could, Gary and Bel nipped round the back of the building. After finding all the doors and windows on the ground floor locked, Gary spotted a ladder that led to the roof. 'Come on!' he said. 'Let's see what's up here.'

'I hate doing dangerous stuff without superpowers,' said Bel. 'We could get into all sorts of trouble.'

'What's the worst that could happen?' asked Gary, already on the ladder.

Bel could think of plenty of things but she followed him anyway.

'You'll be all right,' Gary shouted down to her. It had started to rain though, making the metal rungs of the ladder slippery. Gary didn't seem to notice. Even without his Chimp superpowers he was a nimble and confident climber, but Bel struggled to keep her grip. She almost fell off a few times and by the time she reached the top rung, her heart was pounding.

Gary put out his hand to help her get off the ladder and once Bel was on the roof, her spirits lifted. The roof was flat and there were big circular windows dotted all over it, designed to bring as much daylight into the building as possible.

'We just need to find one of these windows that will open,' said Gary.

'And hope it doesn't set off the alarm,' said Bel.

They sprinted around testing all the window catches until Gary shouted, 'Yes!' He'd found a window with a lock that was already broken so he just prised it up a bit more and stuck his head through the gap. 'Not too far to drop down. Just make sure you miss the ornamental goldfish pond.'

96

Gary and Bel carefully hung from the top of the window and lowered themselves down into the shop. Gary found a dog basket to hide in and Bel buried herself in a cardboard box full of cat toys.

'Don't move until we catch them red-handed,' whispered Gary.

'That's if they show up at all,' said Bel. 'We might be hiding in the wrong pet shop.'

They didn't have to wait much longer to find out.

Round at the front of the shop, Ruby had managed to cheer Morris up by sharing a chunk of chocolate with him.

'An army marches on its stomach and so do Morrises,' said Morris, smiling.

'I know you'd have come up with a brilliant plan with a bit more time,' said Ruby. 'But we were in a rush.'

'And now we're in a bush,' Morris answered.

'How's the chocolate?' asked Ruby.

'**Uggggghhhh**,' yelled Morris.

'That bad? Sorry, it'd been in my bag for a while. Was it covered in fluff?'

'OOOOHHHHH FLIPPING 'ECK, FLIPPING 'ECK, FLIPPING 'ECK.' Morris was shrinking and twitching. As usual, he was the first of the Fish Fingers to feel the transformation coming.

91

'Oh, here we go!' whispered Ruby, starting to tingle herself. For a moment she couldn't see any sign of the crooks but then suddenly Tereza's truck pulled up opposite, with the villain who looked like a chicken nugget sitting on a spoon in front.

KangaRuby ducked down behind the bush as far as she could. It was actually a pretty good hiding place, especially now that Morris was slug-sized.

Stealthily, The Bog Snorkeler, Flunk, Pizza Delivery Girl and Tereza stepped out of the truck to join Zultar.

'It'd be nice to do this job without all the fuss we had last time,' Tereza whispered.

'Yess,' said The Bog Snorkeler. 'We need ssubtlety and ssophistication.'

'I quite agree,' said Zultar, getting out a map of the inside of the shop. 'Here's the plan. Bog Snorkeler, I want you to dive into a drain and come up in the ornamental fishpond. Check there are no guards in the building. Then on your signal, Pizza Delivery Girl will cut the cables on the alarm with a thin and crispy. Finally, a gentle breeze from Tereza's nose should be enough to prise open the doors.'

'Hey, Zultee,' whispered Flunk. 'What shall I do?'

'No messing around this time,' said Zultar. 'Just use your head.' But as soon as the words left his lips, he wished he'd chosen a different expression.

'Will do!' said Flunk and charged horn-first at the thick plate-glass doors. The glass shattered instantly, setting off the alarm and Flunk landed upside down in the ornamental fishpond. 'Shop's open!' he yelled. 'But can somebody help me out? These fish tickle!'

Pizza Delivery Girl sent a thin and crispy (toe cheese and rat spittle) spinning towards the burglar alarm and it sliced through the cables like a razor blade. Sparks flew and the wires fizzed before the alarm suddenly stopped. Then the gang set to work looking for hamsters.

Outside behind the bush, Slug Boy and KangaRuby had a problem. The Slug Mobile was dangling from Nightingale's wrist and she was somewhere in the shop. It meant KangaRuby would have to carry Slug Boy in her hand but he was so slippery, he kept squirming through her fingers and splatting on the ground. KangaRuby had an idea. 'I could carry you in my magic pocket.'

'If you like,' said Slug Boy. So KangaRuby carefully scooped him up with the melted ice-lolly stick and plopped him in.

'What's it like inside there?' she asked.

'Dark,' said Slug Boy. 'But quite snug. I've found a settee to sit on.'

Inside the pet shop, the villains had a hamster cage in each hand (except for Flunk who had six) and they were heading for the exit when Nightingale and The Chimp burst out of their hiding places.

The Chimp shouted, '**Stop right there!** Hand over those hamsters.'

Nightingale said, 'Come quietly now. Of course, you'll still have to go to prison but it'll be much worse if you come noisily.'

Zultar was very confused. There was nothing about Earthlings like these in the *Earth Guide*. He pointed his atomic liquidizer at The Chimp and Nightingale and said, 'I haven't the foggiest idea who you are or what you're talking about.'

Then KangaRuby bounced through the door. 'We're the Fabulous Four Fish Fingers!' she said. 'And, Mr Nugget, you've had your chips!'

'We have you surrounded,' said Slug Boy from deep inside KangaRuby's pocket but nobody could really hear him. KangaRuby dipped her fingers in to pull Slug Boy out but instead she produced a lettuce. Then a coat hanger, a pencil and a two-man tent.

By now Zultar was utterly baffled so Tereza tried to clear things up. 'It's like this. You know how we are the bad guys? Well these chumps are the good guys. And they can spoil a party like a baboon barfing in a birthday cake. There are usually four of them. There'll be a sluggy one somewhere.'

'With or without a sluggy one, the odds seem to be on our side,' said Zultar calmly. He set his atomic liquidizer to **BLAST (IMPRESSIVE)** and aimed it at the Fish Fingers. 'Let me introduce myself,' he said. 'I am Zultar the Magnificent. And you are . . . history!' He fired at the nearest target – The Chimp. Luckily, the superhero ducked in time but the blast made a hole in the wall so big it left mostly hole and not much wall at all. As The Chimp ran for his life, Zultar kept his finger on the trigger, leaving such a trail of blast holes the building began to collapse. The Chimp clambered up a cage full of parrots and hid in the rafters.

KangaRuby was still fishing around inside her pocket for Slug Boy when a deep pan pizza (sour milk and ear wax) dropped out of the sky and smothered her. KangaRuby yelled, 'Get this thing off me!' but Pizza Delivery Girl giggled and said, 'Talk to the hand, it's got a pizza in it. Oh, and by the way, that hat you're wearing, it's like totally ungroovy.'

Nightingale suddenly felt very outnumbered. Five against four had been poor odds but now it was five against one. She hovered in the air and nine evil eyes turned their attention to her.

'Not so long ago, you and your friends were ganging up on me!' said Tereza the Sneezer. 'Now how do *you* like it?'

Nightingale opened her mouth to sing. Her song was the most powerful weapon the Fish Fingers had – it could uproot trees and shake the Earth – but as she uttered her first note, the Bog Snorkeler pointed his trident and blasted her with electricity. Nightingale hung in the air for a second before dropping like a puppet with its strings cut.

'**Nooooo!**' screamed The Chimp, diving down from the rafters to cushion her fall. He caught her before she hit the ground and rolled sideways to protect Nightingale's limp body. But he rolled only as far as Tereza's feet. She bent down and sneezed from point-blank range, covering both superheroes in snotty green goo.

'Well it didn't take too long to defeat them,' said Zultar. 'Flunk, just make sure those two in the goo don't get up. The one in the silly hat looks like she'll be busy eating pizza for a while. And as for the mysterious sluggy one, we haven't even seen him. Well done, Tereza, Bog Snorkeler, Pizza Delivery Girl. Right, let's get these hamsters loaded.'

By the time Slug Boy had found a way out of KangaRuby's pocket and the other Fish Fingers were back on their feet, Zultar's gang had long since escaped. Slug Boy sat miserably on a pile of dog biscuits surveying the damage. It looked like Paws and Claws had been hit by a tornado. Gerbils, mice, guinea pigs and rabbits scurried across the floor, their cages tossed aside as the villains hunted for hamsters. Some of the smaller animals were stuck in puddles of Tereza's green snot, others were escaping through the holes that had been blasted in the walls. Shelves full of pet food had been torn down as Flunk searched for things to eat (his current favourite was cat flea collars). Parrots, budgies and cockatoos fluttered in the rafters or pecked at birdseed on the floor. A particularly big cockatoo spotted something that looked even tastier than birdseed though: Slug Boy. Squawking loudly, it swooped down and opened its beak to snaffle him up but Slug Boy was not in the mood to be bird breakfast. 'Back off, buddy,' he yelled. 'Or I'll pull your tongue so far out of your mouth the gerbils could use it as a skipping rope.' The cockatoo wasn't used to being shouted at by snacks, no matter how tasty-looking, so it flapped off to find something a bit friendlier to eat.

'What a mess,' said The Chimp, scooping Slug Boy into the Slug Mobile. 'I'm glad I'm not the cleaner.'

'And what's that terrible stink?' asked Nightingale.

'I thinks that's the smell of the Bog Snorkeler,' answered KangaRuby. 'It seems to linger in the air.'

'There's something else in the air too,' said Slug Boy. 'The stink of failure. Ours.'

'I think there were just too many of them,' said KangaRuby. 'We'll catch them next time though, you'll see. We just need to think of a better plan.'

'Better than jumping out of a bush,' muttered Slug Boy.

PET SCHOOL

The raids by The Nuggets were front-page news. It turned out Paws and Claws hadn't been their only target during the night. While the Fish Fingers were sleeping off their disastrous defeat, the villains had hit every other pet shop in Tumchester. The owner of a shop called Call Me Cuddles told a reporter, 'I was in bed and suddenly I couldn't breathe. I thought the cat might be sleeping on my head again but I opened my eyes and it was a pizza, topped with Brussels sprouts and anchovies. I hate sprouts and I'm allergic to anchovies. Horrible salty things. By the time I ate my way out, the hamsters had all been stolen. Three hundred of them. Vanished.'

The gang had even raided a farm on the outskirts of the town that *supplied* pet shops with hamsters. Farmer Simon Sniggle had suffered a terrible fate and he told breakfast news, 'A thing that looked like a chicken nugget pointed a spoon at me and said, "It's your hamsters or your life." At first I thought he said, "hamsters or your wife," so I went to get Mavis out of bed but the nugget just blasted a big hole in the floor with his spoon. Then a furry monster held me upside down and a big fish said he'd electrify me unless I told him where the hamsters were. He didn't need to do that. There's a sign up.'

The farmer's interview was followed by a police statement made by Detective Rigley. The statement said, 'I'm very busy investigating so I can't come to the studio. And I haven't had my breakfast yet. But I can confirm that these were copycat attacks by the same gang. And that doesn't mean they are a gang of cats.'

The situation was getting grimmer but the Fish Fingers had to try to put it out of their minds. For a start they couldn't do anything until after school and it was Bring Your Pet to Class Day, a real treat in the calendar. Everybody looked forward to it, except Morris, who hadn't got a pet because his mum didn't really like animals. If he ever asked his mum for a goldfish or even a gerbil, she'd have an excuse like, 'What about when we go on holiday? We'd have to ask the neighbours to look after it. And then afterwards they'd say, 'We took care of your gerbil so you've got to look after our man-eating alligator for a month and **OOH**, can we borrow your lawnmower and can our aunty live in your attic? Not on your nelly.'

Morris decided this year he wasn't going empty-handed to Bring Your Pet to Class Day. He found an empty matchbox and headed into the garden to look for a slug. Unfortunately, he couldn't see any slugs but he did find a woodlouse so he put that in the box with some bark chippings. 'I'll call you **The Beast!**' he said to himself. 'At least it'll give everyone a giggle.'

At 27 Fish Street, Gary was getting Ricky Junior's cage ready for school but he was nervous about the whole thing. It was now very clear that the villains were targeting hamsters so just how safe was Ricky going to be? Until now the gang had only taken hamsters from shops and they hadn't gone anywhere near people's pets. But what if they changed their minds? At that moment a fly buzzed in through the open window and started weaving in and out of the hamster cage. Gary tried to flick it away but the fly wasn't going anywhere. Gary rolled up a comic and swung it like a light sabre but the force seemed to be with the fly. It dodged and weaved, red eyes twinkling like sparks as the young Jedi kept whacking thin air. Eventually the fly whizzed off through the window but as it did, it made a kind of whirring sound.

Stupid fly, Gary thought. But he was wrong. This particular fly was a lot cleverer than it looked.

Morris walked to school on his own that morning because the other Fish Fingers had to transport their pets in proper cages and their mums and dads took them in cars. When Morris arrived at the school gates he noticed Ferret (with his pet ferret) and Snoddy with his big black dog Belcher. Morris had had run-ins with Snoddy's walking set of gnashers before so he waited until it had gone before he went inside.

The classroom was like a petting farm and the walls vibrated with all the clucking, chirruping, purring, barking and squawking. Ruby had brought her parrot Marvin, who was hopping around in his cage yelling, 'MAAAARVIN'SSTAAAAAAAAARRRRVINNNGG!' Bel had brought her cat Cuddles, who didn't seem to mind the noise. She was sleeping in a basket, snuggled up in her own long white fur. Of course, Gary had brought Ricky Junior, who was busy running a marathon on his wheel. Morris sat down and got out his matchbox. It had a picture of the queen on it and Morris had written 'Beware' on the back in felt-tip pen.

The room was certainly as noisy as usual but the mood amongst the class wasn't quite as joyful. The news about the pet-shop raids had affected everybody. After taking the register, Mr Plimsole tried to jolly things along. The children liked him because he was a bit strict but he also liked a joke. Mr Plimsole wore glasses and had little silver wisps around his temples.

'Okay, folks,' he said. 'This is how the lesson will run. I'm going to ask you some questions about your pet and I'll give you a mark out of ten for your knowledge. But I'll also be checking that you really understand what it means to be responsible for another little life. We need to care for our pets, keep them fed, watered and warm so they live happily ever after. There'll be a mark out of ten for a caring attitude too.'

After interviewing most of the children, Mr Plimsole came over to Morris and picked up his matchbox. 'Has your mum changed her mind about you having a pet?' he asked.

'I keep it a secret from her,' said Morris. 'It's because my pet's a killer. Be careful when you open the box, he might bite your arm off.'

'Interesting, what exactly is he?' asked Mr Plimsole with a smile.

'He's a man-eating woodlouse,' said Morris. 'And he's called **The Beast!**'

Tentatively, Mr Plimsole opened the box and peered inside. 'Twiddle, there's nothing in here except bark chippings.' The woodlouse had long since scarpered and everybody giggled. It was just what they all needed to take their minds off the hamster snatchers.

'The Beast might have turned invisible,' said

Morris. 'He does that sometimes.'

Mr Plimsole tipped the contents of the matchbox onto Morris's desk. 'No, I think he's simply chosen freedom over captivity.'

'Impossible!' said Morris. 'He wouldn't have left without saying goodbye.' Mr Plimsole laughed and Morris saw it as a sign that he could carry on. He turned round to make sure Gary was laughing first though. That was the most important thing. Gary was chuckling louder than anybody else so Morris pretended to burst into tears. 'I can't believe he's left me like this. He was my best friend.'

'I thought Gamble over there was your best friend,' said the teacher.

'Gary's my best friend on Earth, Mr Plimsole. But The Beast is from a galaxy far far away. Actually, even further away than that. You have to turn left at a galaxy far far away and keep going past the newsagents.'

'He's gone then,' said Mr Plimsole. 'But whenever you look up at a starry sky, remember, he's out there. Shall I throw the box in the bin?'

'No, I'll keep it in my pocket to help me remember the life we could have had, *should* have had,' said Morris. By now Gary's sides were aching because he was laughing so much. So was everybody else (except Snoddy and Ferret who were busy flicking each other's ears and seeing who could pinch the other's leg the hardest). Morris was delighted.

'Very good, Twiddle. Ten out of ten for imagination,' said Mr Plimsole. 'However, zero out of ten for your pet and your caring attitude. Now, let's get on with picking a winner!'

Top score eventually went to Ruby, whose parrot knowledge was long and deep and it was clear that she took great care of Marvin. He proudly rang his bell to celebrate. Ruby's prize was a fridge magnet in the shape of giraffe, which was quite cute and she shoved it in her trouser pocket.

At the end of the session, all the mums and dads came in to school to collect the pets and the children went off to eat in the canteen.

'Mozza, you were so funny this morning,' said Gary, tucking into a tuna sandwich. 'I don't know how you come out with it.'

'You do make me laugh, Morris,' said Bel.

'I'll have to try and remember everything you said so I can tell my gran,' said Ruby.

Morris blushed. He liked a bit of attention but not too much because he got embarrassed. 'Let's, er, get down to business then,' he said. 'The pet shops. Which one do you think we should stake out next?'

'There aren't any left in Tumchester that haven't been raided,' said Bel. 'I googled it last night.'

'Well what about the zoo then?' said Ruby.

Morris raised an eyebrow. 'There are lions at the zoo, yes. Tigers, orang-utans, elephants and chimpanzees, yes. But cages full of hamsters? I don't think so!'

'So what do you think the gang'll do next?' asked Gary. 'You don't think they'd ever try to steal pets from, you know, kids' bedrooms, do you?'

'No, no,' said Bel.

'Good gravy no,' said Ruby.

'Absolutely not,' said Morris. 'These villains are horrid but they aren't **THAT** horrid.' Unfortunately, Morris was wrong. Very wrong.

ROCKING AND ROLLING

At the hideout Zultar was deep in a 4D hologram conversation with his mum.

'You haven't kept the hideout very tidy,' said the Great Elder. 'It could do with a good clean. But good work on completing phase one of the mission. You should begin phase two tonight. And make sure you don't leave any hamsters behind. Showing no mercy is the sign of a true intergalactic superpower. And how's your brother?'

'Oh, you know Flunk. His usual self,' said Zultar.

'Excellent,' said the Great Elder. 'Make sure you keep him out of harm's way. Then all being well, I'll see you tomorrow. I'll ask your dad to make something nice for tea.'

The Great Elder signed off and Zultar went to the control room to hold a meeting. Tereza was there already, stroking her nose like it was a kitten. Then the Bog Snorkeler arrived (coming via the toilet as usual) and he sat dripping filthy water onto the carpet. A few minutes later Pizza Delivery Girl stomped in saying, 'No way am I sitting next to Mr Stink Bomb Pants again. It doesn't matter how many pegs I put on my nose.'

'Sso nice and polite,' said The Bog Snorkeler.

'Whatever,' said Pizza Delivery Girl.

'Er, has anyone seen Flunk?' asked Zultar. Nobody had. Zultar was about to call his brother over the intercom again when Flunk staggered in holding his tummy. It looked like he'd swallowed a grand piano.

'Bit poorly,' Flunk said. He told them he'd been in the cargo room looking after the hamsters when he'd felt a bit peckish and popped into the kitchen. After eating the entire contents of the fridge (including the little plastic tray for making ice cubes) he'd gone outside to look for snacks around Wiggy's Bottom. Unfortunately, all he could see were rocks and sheep and he didn't fancy tucking into a sheep so he began chewing on what was left. Soon he'd eaten so many rocks he could hardly move.

'Tummy . . . aches . . .' said Flunk. 'They looked so . . . tasty.'

'What on Nrrmmff made you eat rocks?' asked Zultar.

'Daddy makes the best rock cakes ever,' said Flunk. 'I figured if rocks taste so nice in a cake, they must be pretty good on their own. And they were okay. But I think I may have eaten too many.'

'For the record, Dad doesn't put real rocks in . . . oh, forget it,' said Zultar, pressing on with the meeting. '**It is time for phase two of our mission**. Tonight we'll focus on the hamsters kids keep in their bedrooms.'

'But there must be hundreds of them!' said Tereza.

'In Tumchester there are exactly one hundred and twenty-four,' said Zultar.

'How do you know?' asked the Bog Snorkeler.

'Flies,' said Zultar.

Flunk immediately checked the zip on his trousers.

'Not trouser flies,' said Zultar. He pressed a button on the table and out popped a silver box containing two shiny bluebottles with red eyes. 'Thanks to these Fact-Finding-Flies we now know the exact location of every single pet hamster in Tumchester, as well as their names, the names of their owners, their ages and even what they had for tea.'

'I had rocks for my tea,' said Flunk. 'I'm not going to do that again.'

Then Zultar explained the plan. It was despicable. Even the despicable villains around the table were appalled by its despicableness.

'Make no mistake,' said Zultar, 'these raids will cause the biggest outrage Tumchester has ever seen. Tonight we're not stealing nameless hamsters from shops. We're robbing real pets with names like Nibbles and Cookie from their own homes, so the

Earthlings won't like it one bit. Still, no pain no gain. Any questions?'

'Can we take a picnic?' asked Flunk. 'But not rocks. I think I might be allergic to them.'

As soon as it was dark, the crooks began in the north of the city. Tereza drove *Fnunderbride* slowly down a road called Dingle View with Zultar riding on the roof. The back doors of the truck were open so that Flunk, Pizza Delivery Girl and the Bog Snorkeler could dash out, hunting for hamsters. They all carried lists of their hamster targets and pens so they could tick them off one by one. Zultar began the destruction by blasting his atomic liquidizer at as many cars as he could to cause mass confusion. When all the mums and dads rushed out to see what was going on, the villains raided their homes and stole their hamsters.

The first creature on Pizza Delivery Girl's list was Nibbles and it belonged to a boy called Charlie Finch. While Charlie's parents stood in the street crying over the crumpled mess that was once their car, Pizza Delivery Girl sneaked round the back of their house and went in through the patio doors.

Charlie kept his hamster in the living room and he was sitting guarding him with a plastic sword.

'Hey, kid, wanna pizza?' asked Pizza Delivery Girl.

'Yes please,' said Charlie, thinking nobody who was offering pizza could possibly want to steal his hamster. 'But don't tell my mum. She says I shouldn't eat too many and I had one for my tea.'

'Mums talk a lot of nonsense' said Pizza Delivery Girl, whipping up a deep pan that was so big it covered Charlie Finch from head to foot and she smothered him in it. He didn't know whether to laugh or cry. Or eat. He decided to eat, but by the time Charlie had chewed a hole in his pizza (dandruff and bread mould flavour) Nibbles and the cage were gone.

Laura Dimple's pet Bubbles fell victim to Zultar. He leapt off the truck and blasted a hole in Laura's front door before bounding up the stairs. By now word had spread, and Zultar found Laura's dad handcuffed to the hamster cage. 'You aren't getting our Bubbles,' he yelled. 'Not without me!'

Laura and her mum were standing there too, armed with garden spades.

'Just clear off,' said Laura's mum.

'You're a very naughty nugget,' shouted Laura.

Zultar smiled. Then he set his atomic liquidizer to **_BALLOON (HEADS)_** and blasted Laura and her mum. The effect was instant and very freaky. Their heads grew bigger and stretchier until they looked like giant watermelons and they lifted gently off the ground. Soon they were bobbing around the ceiling.

'Get us down,' they shrieked.

Zultar stared coldly into Laura's dad's eyes. 'Either you give me the hamster or I'll open a window and you can watch your wife and daughter drift outside on the night air. It's quite windy so I estimate they'll be in North Africa by tomorrow morning. If their balloon heads haven't been popped by a pigeon before then.'

Tears rolling down his cheeks, Laura's dad unlocked his handcuffs from the hamster cage and handed it over. 'Just horrid, that's what you are,' he said, grabbing his wife and Laura by their trouser legs.

'The effect should wear off in a couple of days,' shouted Zultar as he ran off with Bubbles. 'Then again, it might not.'

Two houses down, Tommy Thompson was kissing his hamster Cookie goodnight when he heard his dad shout something from the bathroom. Tommy ran to see what was wrong and found that the Bog Snorkeler had come up through the bath where his dad had been having a soak. The Bog Snorkeler had jammed his dad's toe up the cold tap and the poor man lay there in the bubbles, unable to move. The Bog Snorkeler spotted Cookie in Tommy's hand. 'Ssso kind of you to bring your hamster to me, sssaves me the trouble of looking for him.'

Tommy tried to run but the Bog Snorkeler snatched the animal from his hand and jumped out through the bathroom window before Tommy could even scream.

Flunk found he wasn't very good at snatching hamsters. He hated making the little Earthlings cry. The first hamster on his list was called Peepo and when he arrived at the address, he ran through the front door and bashed his way into Lucy Diddle's bedroom. She was sitting on her bed in her pyjamas with her blond hair tied in two little plaits.

'Hi,' she said. 'I'm Lucy. Are you the new babysitter?'

'Er, yes,' said Flunk. 'I'm a hamster babysitter. I've come to look after Peepo.'

'He's very friendly,' said Lucy. 'He'll even run around inside your pyjamas and pop out the top and then sit on your head. Just watch.' Lucy took the little animal out of his cage and set him on her hand. Sure enough, Peepo wriggled his way into the sleeve of her pyjamas and ran up her arm until he peeped out of the collar. Then he scrambled up one of her plaits, sat on top of her head and settled down for a snooze.

It was the cutest thing Flunk had ever seen. On Nrrmmff, hamsters were working animals. But here on Earth it was different somehow.

'Lucy, I, er, have to go now,' Flunk said. 'I'm really sorry but I can't babysit your hamster tonight. I'll have to leave him here with you.'

'Can't you stay and play for a bit?' she asked.

Flunk shook his head, gave Lucy a little wave and dashed through the hole where the door used to be.

When he got back to the truck he found his brother wasn't in a touchy-feely kind of mood. 'We haven't got time for sob stories!' Zultar yelled. 'Don't you remember our planet's on its last legs? We need hamsters and we need them fast. We're doing something a little bit bad so that we achieve something very very good.'

'But . . . but,' said Flunk.

'No buts. From now on, you can drive the truck. I'll get Tereza to snatch the hamsters off your list.'

Although Tereza wasn't very happy about Flunk driving she made a much better hamster kidnapper than he did. The first thing she did was go back to Lucy Diddle's house and after blowing her bedroom apart with a powerful sneeze, she quickly snatched Peepo and his cage.

Now the gang started making fast progress through the streets. The Bog Snorkeler swam as though his life depended on it. Up the U-bends, round the pipes, sometimes popping out in shower cubicles, bidets, hot tubs or washing machines, anywhere there was a pipe and a water supply. His favourite route remained lavatories though and he didn't care whether they were occupied or not. If they were empty, it made his job easier. If they were in use, it simply gave him a nice, round target for his electric trident.

When the raids began, the Fish Fingers were asleep in their beds. The first robberies had taken place in the far north of Tumchester, too far away to trigger their superhero transformations. But as Tereza's truck drove closer to Fish Street, the children woke up and felt their bodies tingle with superpower.

Nightingale fluttered round to Slug Boy's bedroom to collect him and they zoomed down Fish Street to find KangaRuby and The Chimp. Nightingale did a quick sweep over the rooftops and soon spotted the crooks. 'It looks like they're kidnapping hamsters street by street,' she said.

'So they're really stealing hamsters from . . . homes?' asked The Chimp. 'How do they know where the hamsters live?'

'Dunno,' said Slug Boy. 'But they seem to. And that means Ricky Junior's not safe. Let's get to your house and hide him. That way at least . . .' But Slug Boy didn't have time to finish what he was saying. The roar of an engine told them that Tereza's truck was already in Fish Street.

'I'll try to do something to stall them,' said KangaRuby. 'You save Ricky Junior.'

Zultar jumped up onto the roof of *Fnunderbride* and blasted as many parked cars as he could. As usual, it brought angry and confused crowds onto the street. Some of them tried to stand in front of the truck, but Tereza just sneezed and blew them back into their gardens, with a layer of green goo for good measure.

Standing at Gary's garden gate, KangaRuby

dipped her hand into her magic pocket in the hope of finding something useful. She pulled out a plate of mince pies, a frozen turkey and a stocking. *Perfect, if only I was planning a Christmas party*, she thought. But then she had an idea. KangaRuby shoved the turkey down into the stocking and started to swing it round her head. As it gained speed she let it fly and it smashed the windscreen of the truck.

Flunk leapt out. He wasn't happy. Especially as Zultar would say it was his fault. He spotted KangaRuby and made a beeline for her, but KangaRuby still had the mince pies. As Flunk approached, she took a nibble of one and Flunk could tell it was really tasty. His nostrils filled with the smell of raisins, currants and pastry.

'These are great,' said KangaRuby, who'd remembered this supervillain had a very healthy appetite from the pet shop. 'Fancy one?'

Flunk checked that Zultar wasn't watching. 'Yes I do, yes I do, yes I do,' he said.

'You can have the whole plate,' said KangaRuby. 'But you have to chew them really slowly and stay in one place, or, or you turn into a very smelly jellyfish.'

'Wow, thanks for the tip!' said Flunk and as he stood eating the delicious pies, KangaRuby dashed off to find the others.

Unfortunately, while KangaRuby had been taking

care of Flunk, the Bog Snorkeler had slipped into a nearby drain and popped out of Gary's toilet while Gary's dad was sitting on it. Now the poor man was staggering around the bathroom, hair standing on end, body fizzing like a firework and the Bog Snorkeler was on his way to Gary's bedroom.

When KangaRuby got upstairs, she discovered Nightingale, Slug Boy and The Chimp trying to fight the Bog Snorkeler. Or at least, trying to fight his overpowering stench. He was wafting his whiff around Gary's bedroom and the Fish Fingers were on their knees. (Well, Slug Boy would have been on his knees if he'd had any knees.) The bedroom windows were shut and the room was small so it meant the stink had no way to escape. The superheroes found their eyelids getting heavy and their heads starting to swim. The Bog Snorkeler had Ricky Junior's cage under his arm.

KangaRuby quickly put her hand in her pocket and pulled out a cabbage. She flung it towards the Bog Snorkeler and it zipped past his ear.

'Misssed by miless,' he sneered. 'Now, if you'll excusse me, I have a hamsster to ssteal.'

But KangaRuby's cabbage hadn't missed its target at all. It had smashed the window she'd been aiming for and fresh air now flooded into the room.

The Bog Snorkeler threatened KangaRuby with his

trident. 'Keep your fingersss where I can ssee them,' he said. 'If they go near that pocket again, you'll be ssizzlling like a ssaussage on a sskewer.'

The Bog Snorkeler turned to leave but as he did so, The Chimp somersaulted across the floor, picking up his bedroom telly as he went and he smashed it down on the Bog Snorkeler's head.

'What's it like to be on TV?' asked The Chimp.

As the villain staggered, Nightingale grabbed him by the flippers and pulled his legs from under him. KangaRuby tried to catch Ricky Junior's cage as it fell from the Bog Snorkeler's grasp but it bounced onto the floor and the door swung open. Ricky Junior made a dash for it. He sprinted one way, then the other with the Fish Fingers all trying to grab him but the hamster was too quick for them. Daintily, he scampered behind a cupboard and disappeared into a hole in the floorboards. He was now somewhere underneath them. They could hear his little feet, tippety tapping but they couldn't see him.

The Bog Snorkeler's head was clearing. With the Fish Fingers distracted, he decided it was time to get reinforcements. He darted into the bathroom and dived into the lavatory, yelling, '**Sso long, ssuckersss**.'

In the bedroom, The Chimp remembered there was a bit of carpet by the door that wasn't quite

127

stuck to the floorboards. He gave it a tug, revealing the bare wood underneath. KangaRuby put her hand in her pocket, searching for something to help. She pulled out: a hot dog, a goldfish bowl, a coat hanger, a duck, a whoopee cushion, a lawnmower and a jar of coleslaw. The Chimp grabbed the coat hanger and used the hook to dig into the floorboard and pull it up. Ricky Junior's nose peeped up through the hole but then he disappeared again. Nightingale was standing guard at the other hole and that's where Ricky Junior poked his nose out next.

'Come on, little fella,' she said but Ricky Junior seemed to be enjoying himself. He dashed out of the hole, hurdled brilliantly over Nightingale's fingers and ran under the bed. The real Ricky Zigzag would have been proud.

Slug Boy had an idea and he told Nightingale to take the Slug Mobile off her wrist and pop it under the bed with the lid off. Puzzled, she did as she was asked.

'Come in here, Ricky, with me, come on,' Slug Boy whispered to the hamster. The hamster figured it looked safe enough. It wasn't exactly his home cage but the funny-looking thing inside seemed friendly enough. With a twitch of his nose, Ricky Junior leapt inside the Slug Mobile and Slug Boy flipped the door shut.

Just then the Fish Fingers heard footsteps on the stairs. The Bog Snorkeler was coming back and he'd brought Tereza, Zultar and Pizza Delivery Girl with him. Ricky Junior was the last hamster on their list – the last hamster in Tumchester – and the crooks were not going to leave him behind.

Desperately, KangaRuby reached under the bed and picked up the Slug Mobile. As the supervillains charged into the room, KangaRuby slipped the Slug Mobile on her wrist and leapt out of the window, swiftly followed by Nightingale and The Chimp.

Zultar was about to follow them but the sound of police sirens outside made him stop. 'Forget it, for now,' he said to his gang. 'But we'll be back.'

KangaRuby and The Chimp were running as fast as they could along Fish Street, and Nightingale was flying overhead. A line of police cars screeched past them, sirens blaring, red lights flashing. Everywhere cars were on fire and angry residents were trying to put out the flames. Children who'd lost their hamsters were crying and being cuddled by their parents. The Fish Fingers turned to see if the supervillains were chasing after them.

'I can't see them anywhere,' said The Chimp.

'Maybe the police have got them,' said Nightingale.

'I hope so,' said KangaRuby.

'I wouldn't bet on it,' said Slug Boy. 'Those villains are despicable, disgusting and . . . **UGH**, Ricky Junior's just done his business in the bottom of my Slug Mobile.'

I SPY

When their superpowers had worn off, the Fish Fingers made their way back to Fish Street with Ricky Junior in the Slug Mobile. It had been a dark, dark night. Gary's house was the first one they came to and just as Gary was saying, 'See ya,' to Ruby, Bel and Morris, a tall man stepped out of the bushes. He had coal black hair and sunglasses and he was wearing a bright yellow jacket. 'Gary Gamble?' he said. 'I need you to come with me.'

'No chance,' said Gary. 'I never go anywhere with strangers.'

'None of us do,' said Bel.

'Don't you ever watch TV?' asked Morris. 'It's a mad, bad world out there.'

The man flashed a badge. 'My name is Agent Joe Lemon and I'm from the M25. Have you heard of the M25?'

'Yes, it's a big motorway,' said Ruby. 'We use it when we go on holiday.'

'Er, yes, the M25 is a motorway I admit. But it's

also the name of a top-secret organisation,' said the agent. 'Have you ever heard of the *top secret* M25?'

'No,' said Ruby.

'Good,' said Lemon. 'If you had, I'd have needed to arrest you for breaching national security. That's how top secret we are. My own mother doesn't know I'm a secret agent. She thinks I'm a carpet fitter.'

'If you're a secret agent, why are you wearing such a jazzy jacket?' asked Ruby. 'You stick out a mile.'

'I know and it's really annoying for a spy,' admitted Agent Lemon. 'Unfortunately that's our uniform. I keep telling my boss it should be black but he won't listen.'

'Are you here to do security for the Trophy Games?' asked Gary.

'Right salad, wrong cucumber,' said Agent Lemon.

'Er, pardon?' said Gary.

'At the M25 we only deal with extra-terrestrial infiltration.'

'Extra . . . what?' asked Gary, who was still trying to work out what the salad and the cucumbers had to do with anything.

'I'm talking about aliens, sonny,' said Agent Lemon. 'We're the guys people talk to if they've seen flying saucers, little green men or Martians from outer space. A hundred times out of a hundred it's a false alarm. But we have reason to believe there's now been genuine contact from alien beings. Gary, I need to ask you some questions in total privacy and the future of every hamster on the planet could be in your hands. Now, please follow me to my helicopter.'

'Only if my friends can come too,' said Gary.

Agent Lemon thought for a moment then pushed an earpiece into his ear and spoke into the lapel of his coat. 'Agent Lemon here. Will escort target to location for questioning. And er, target is bringing his mates.'

The Fish Fingers followed Agent Lemon along Fish Street to the school field and he led them across the playground towards the football pitch. The children were starting to feel the hairs on the back of their necks stand on end. Agent Lemon spoke into his lapel once more and suddenly a light came on in the helicopter cockpit; it had been parked on the pitch all along but somehow none of them had spotted it.

'That is **AWESOME!**' said Gary.

'Stealth technology, son,' said Agent Lemon. 'I never leave home without it. Now, step aboard.'

Once the children were seated in the helicopter, Agent Lemon asked, 'Have you ever heard of COSMIC DUST?'

They shook their heads.

'It comes from the furthest reaches of the known

universe,' said Agent Lemon. 'Until recently there were just a few grains of it on Earth, collected from space by our most secret interstellar probe. But three days ago our cosmic-dust monitoring machines went bonkers. They detected a build-up of cosmic dust in Tumchester High Street where a bunch of traffic cones had been melted. The same cosmic dust was later found at Big Momma's, Friends Fur-ever, Paws and Claws and every other pet shop that has been raided this week. Last night was final confirmation. Our cosmic-dust detectors were blown off the scale! Aliens are here and they've got our hamsters.'

'Are you sure they aren't just a gang of supervillains?' asked Bel.

'Some of them are supervillains, yes, but two of the gang haven't shown up on any of our global databases: that's the nuggety one and the big furry one. It's like they fell from the sky. Or to put it more simply, dropped from another planet.'

'But why steal hamsters?' asked Bel.

'We're not sure yet, but let me tell you, these guys definitely do not come in peace,' said Agent Lemon. 'Now, Gary's is the only hamster left in Tumchester. That makes it highly valuable and I don't think the aliens will go home without it. Gary, we need to use him to trap these monsters. I need your permission to take, er, what's his name?

'Ricky Junior.'

'Yep, Rocky Junior. I need your permission to take Rocky fishing for aliens and we'll use him as bait.'

'It's Ricky, not Rocky, by the way,' said Gary. 'You know, like the famous runner. And when you say *bait* you don't mean like a maggot on a hook, do you?' Gary didn't like the sound of it.

'No, not like that!' said Agent Lemon. 'Maggots get it right through the wazoobee and then get eaten by a fish. We'll protect Rocky Junior with every weapon we have: stun guns, torpedoes, submarines, fighter jets, tanks. Trust us, we're the experts.'

'Okay,' said Gary. 'You have my permission. But you keep calling him Rocky Junior and it's Ricky Junior, like Ricky Zigzag, the hurdler.'

'Sorry,' said Agent Lemon. 'I'll make a note of that. Now, the next thing we need to do is organise Rocky's transport to a safe place.'

'Where will that be?' asked Morris.

'In the vault at Tumchester Central Bank,' said Lemon. 'The aliens are bound to make an attack but they won't use force to blast open the vault as they clearly want him alive. They'll probably come up with a cunning plan. But we'll have an even more cunning plan and that's how we will catch them!'

Suddenly Agent Lemon noticed a fly buzzing around the helicopter. It seemed to have twinkling red eyes. Lemon tried to swat it, but the fly made a whirring sound and flew off.

DON'T BANK ON IT

At five o'clock the next morning Ricky Junior and his cage were transported by an M25 helicopter to the Tumchester Central Bank and placed in the vault. Agent Lemon's cunning plan turned out to be surrounding the bank with every single troop and every single weapon he could lay his hands on. There were thousands of men and women dressed in bright yellow combat uniforms with the logo 'M25' written on the back. (It was in very small writing because it was supposed to be top secret.) On the Fish Street School field there were fighter jets and there was even a submarine in the River Tum equipped with ground-to-air missiles, an infra-red tracking system, a dishwasher and its own chocolate fountain. On the grassy verges opposite the bank the M25 marksmen were hidden inside trenches with their stun-gun barrels poking out of the top. Other troops were under cars, behind hedges and on top of bus shelters. Inside the bank there were twelve highly trained guards. These were the best of the M25's best and they stood watching a video screen showing live pictures of Ricky Junior from thirty-seven different cameras. The door to the vault was made of the strongest titanium and it couldn't be blown apart or drilled. Opening it required the numbers to a combination lock, known only to one of the guards and a key, which was held by another.

Agent Lemon sat outside in a van that had satellite dishes on the roof and he had a clear view of the bank's front door. *Troops all on red alert. Everybody in position. Good. Could be a pay rise in this for me,* he thought.

At Ruby's house, the Fish Fingers watched everything on TV. They didn't like being so far away because, if anything dangerous happened, it might not trigger their superhero transformations. But Agent Lemon had warned them, 'You kids need to stay home and leave this to the experts.'

After five minutes watching the TV pictures, Gary had had enough. 'We've got to get down there,' he said. 'I'm going stir crazy.'

'But remember Agent Lemon —' said Bel.

'I know what he said,' Gary interrupted. 'But we're superheroes and there's probably going to be an emergency and we just need to be there.'

The others nodded.

'Meet me out front in ten minutes. We'll go on bikes.'

A short time later, the children pedalled into town and parked up about three streets away from the bank. It wasn't as close as they'd have liked but there were barriers up, police cars and the M25 soldiers who were stopping anyone getting too close. The Fish Fingers found a bench to sit on by a TV shop so they could watch events unfold. But it was a slow morning. For five hours nothing happened.

As lunchtime came, all the troops had a break for something to eat. A delivery driver on a motorbike from Big Momma's arrived at a barricade near the back of the bank. He was stopped by a guard, but when he said the order had been made by Agent Lemon, the guard waved him through. As the motorbike went past the barricade, Zultar gave a little snigger. Safe inside his brilliant hiding place, he just couldn't help it.

The driver soon arrived at the back door of the bank. He rang the bell and a tall woman with bulging muscles called Agent Twiffle opened it just a crack. 'Yes,' she said.

'Hi, I've got twelve Happy Meals with chicken nuggets,' said the delivery man. 'Ordered by Agent Lemon.'

'Oh, if the boss asked for it, then it must be okay,'

said Agent Twiffle. She came out and took the tray of drinks first, but as she did so Agent Lemon himself walked around the corner.

'Hold it right there,' he said. 'Happy Meals with nuggets you say? I don't think so!' Agent Lemon spoke into his walkie-talkie. 'It is a code 709. I repeat 7-0-9. Driver, stand back from your vehicle.'

Immediately, there was a loud whistling in the sky and everybody looked up to see a silver torpedo flash through the clouds then smash into the side of the delivery bike, exploding with so much force there was nothing left except black dust and thick smoke. When the smoke cleared, Agent Lemon, Agent Twiffle and the delivery driver had dust all over their faces.

'I never placed an order for Happy Meals,' said Agent Lemon. 'It must have been an alien attempt to infiltrate the bank.'

'Well done, boss,' said Agent Twiffle, wiping her face with a hanky. 'Do you think that one of the nuggets in those happy meals was . . . that nuggety alien then?'

'That is my suspicion, yes. We'll only know for sure when we have done a full forensic test.' said Agent Lemon. 'But back to your position. There could be more attacks. Delivery driver, you'll need to go home on the bus.'

Agent Twiffle realised she was still holding the drinks tray. 'Can I take these?' she asked. 'We're getting really thirsty inside.'

'Sure,' said Agent Lemon, as he headed back to his van with the satellite dishes on the roof.

Twiffle walked into the bank and Zultar shivered. It had been a close call. Lucky for him, nobody had checked the Big Momma cola, where Zultar was bobbing under the surface, using a straw as a snorkel.

A few minutes later, having slurped their drinks, the guards threw their empty cups in the recycling bin and resumed their watch on the video feed from the vault. All was as it should be. Ricky Junior had been on his wheel for most of the morning but he was obviously tired now and he was having a snooze. Inside the recycling bin, Zultar breathed a sigh of relief. The Fact-Finding-Flies had given him all the data he needed about Agent Lemon's trap. Now he was ready to put the rest of the plan into action.

At Wiggy's Bottom, the gang of supervillains checked their watches. 'Time to go,' said Tereza. They started to head for the door but Tereza stopped Flunk. 'Hang on, not you. Zultar gave us very strict instructions to leave you at home, just in case.'

'Just in case of what?' said Flunk.

'In casse the copss ssniff out the hideout,' said

The Bog Snorkeler.

'And in case you do something really dumb at the bank,' said Pizza Delivery Girl.

'And in case you get hungry and start chewing the seats in my truck again!' said Tereza. 'There are in fact about a million different reasons. So stay put. Just in case.' The others piled into Tereza's truck and left Flunk sitting on his own.

At the bank, Zultar sneaked out of the bin and checked that the guards were all watching the video screen. Then he set his atomic liquidizer to **FREEZE (ICY)** and pointed it at the lock on the vault. It sent a silent stream of icy particles into the keyhole. The metal in the lock expanded and the mechanism jammed. Next, Zultar set his atomic liquidizer to **TV SHOW (SUPERHEROES)**. He'd spent the night making a film with 4D holograms of the Fish Fingers on a background that looked exactly like the vault. All the data he needed had been gathered by the Fact-Finding-Flies and his finished work was a blockbuster. He pulled the trigger and it was transmitted into the CCTV cameras and from there it beamed out to every TV in Tumchester and beyond.

Suddenly Agent Twiffle saw three figures dart across the screen. One seemed to be wearing a plastic box on her wrist with a slimy black thing inside.

'Hey, is somebody in the vault?' she shouted.

The other guards frantically checked the video feed. One of them jabbed a button to see a new camera angle. There was no mistaking.

'How in the name of sweet baby cheeses did they get in there?' yelled Agent Twiffle. She shoved in her earpiece and spoke into her lapel. 'Er, we have a problem. Three unidentified intruders wearing masks and purple tracksuits are in the vault. One of them has a box with a possible slug in it.'

'I can see them!' yelled Lemon. 'They probably drilled through the wall or the ceiling or something! Get in there! Now!'

Agent Twiffle punched the numbers into the combination lock and her second in command, a silver-haired agent called Bobbins, turned the key. But the lock wouldn't budge. Agent Bobbins desperately tried again but still, nothing. The mechanism was frozen.

'Did you put in the right combination?' asked Bobbins.

Twiffle got out a piece of paper with the numbers on she kept in case of emergencies.

'**0, 7, 5** . . . hang on that's my auntie's telephone number. She pulled out another piece of paper. 'This is it. **8, 4, 3, 9, 6, 0, 1**,' and she tried the numbers again. 'That's exactly what I did the first time. I knew I'd got it right!' But the key still wouldn't budge and by now the screen showed the intruders had got the hamster in their hands.

Sitting in the TV shop opposite the bank, the Fish Fingers couldn't believe what they were seeing and as they watched, they started to transform.

'It must be Zultar and the rest of them, in disguise' said The Chimp. 'And now they've got Ricky Junior.' He was fighting back tears. 'Agent Lemon has let us down.'

'We've got to get in there. Now!' said Nightingale.

'We'll need to be careful though,' said KangaRuby. 'Because the M25 might think we're the bad guys.'

'There's no might about it,' said Slug Boy. 'We have just become public enemy number one.'

They dashed off as quickly as they could.

Agent Twiffle yelled into her microphone again. 'Agent Lemon, sir, we still can't open the vault and . . .' Her voice tailed off. As she watched the video screen the figures in purple tracksuits seemed to morph into dazzling beams of light and vanish with Ricky Junior's cage. 'Er, Agent Lemon, sir, we have an even bigger problem. They seem to have escaped.'

Just then there was a huge bang outside. It was the noise of a large truck ploughing into the front of the bank and smashing into bricks, timber and plaster.

'Twiffle, you and the rest of the guards get outside now,' said Agent Lemon. 'I think their getaway truck has arrived and we're going to need all the help we can get.'

Inside the bank, Zultar waited for the last agent to leave and then he climbed calmly out of the recycling bin again and went over to the vault. He stood on a chair to reach the combination lock and punched in the numbers he'd heard Agent Twiffle read out. Then he warmed the keyhole gently with his atomic liquidizer, turned the key that had been left in the door and as the vault swung open, he strolled inside and picked up Ricky Junior's cage. Then he hopped on board his atomic liquidizer and headed for the back door.

A NARROW ESCAPE

At the front of the bank, it was like a scene from a war movie. When Tereza's truck had crashed into the entrance, dozens of M25 soldiers had opened fire with water cannons, stun guns, rubber bullets and rocket launchers, but they didn't dent *Fnunderbride*. Even the tyres on Tereza's truck were unscratched; the only thing that could have punctured them was a 50,000-degree laser and the M25 didn't have one of those. As soon as the guns stopped, Pizza Delivery Girl leapt out of the truck, throwing five large pizzas (with worm vomit and sewage) into the air. They made such great targets the marksmen had to shoot but as they raised their stun guns, Pizza Delivery Girl sent a torrent of tomato sauce at the troops. Instantly they started slipping, sliding and falling over like circus clowns in a custard-pie factory.

Tereza jumped out of the truck and had to dodge a helicopter that was flying in to land. She gave her pepper pots a huge shake and unleashed one of the biggest sneezes of her life. The helicopter was blown so far off course it crash-landed in the River Tum and the pilot had to bail out, covered in slimy snot and wishing he'd closed his window. The Bog Snorkeler decided that his best weapon would be sneakiness and he dived down the nearest manhole cover. Seconds later, he popped out of another manhole just behind a platoon of agents and blasted them with his trident.

'I hope Zultar hurriessss up,' shouted the Bog Snorkeler to Tereza. 'We can't keep this many agentss busssy on our own.'

'Ditto that,' Tereza said. 'I can't keep sneezing forever. Zultar doesn't understand what my poor nose has to go through!'

'He's got literally one more minute then I'm like so out of here,' Pizza Delivery Girl shouted.

Then as Tereza dodged another missile that whistled past her hat she yelled, 'Right, that's it. We can wait in the van. Everybody inside.' The three crooks dived into *Fnunderbride* and shut the doors.

'We'll be ssssafe in here,' said the Bog Snorkeler, who was now so nervous he was giving off a stench that made him put a peg over his *own* nose.

Zultar smiled as he watched from his hiding place: an old cardboard box big enough for both him and the hamster cage. He'd told the rest of the gang to keep the M25 troops busy while he grabbed the hamster and said he'd whisk them away in a tractor beam as soon as he was out. But he'd been lying. That had never been part of the plan. He poked a small hole in the cardboard box and aimed his atomic liquidizer at Tereza's truck, setting his weapon to **LASER (50,000 DEGREES)**. He pulled the trigger four times – once for each tyre – and chuckled to himself. 'Zultar, you're a genius!'

Seconds later he heard *Fnunderbride*'s engines roar, he saw the exhaust pipe belch thick fumes and then he heard a yell from inside the truck. It wasn't going anywhere. It couldn't with four punctures. Immediately, agents from the M25 moved in to make their arrests.

'We have you surrounded,' shouted Agent Lemon. 'Come out with your arms in the air. Except for the Bog Snorkeler. If he puts his arms in the air we'll all have to smell his pongy armpits so he must keep his arms down.'

The doors to *Fnunderbride* slid open and the M25 agents rushed in with handcuffs (and nose-cuffs for Tereza, not to mention air freshener for The Bog Snorkeler).

'You'll be going to prison for a very long time,' said Agent Lemon.

'Whatever,' said Pizza Delivery Girl, who started

texting her lawyer.

Then Agent Lemon spotted something on the roof of the bank. It was the Fish Fingers. 'There are the rest of the villains! The ones who nabbed the hamster!' he yelled. 'Attention! All available M25 agents, head for the roof!'

He touched a button on his wristwatch and it switched to computer mode. Data flashed up on the screen. 'Targets are a group known as the Fabulous Four Fish Fingers. Previously thought to be superheroes, they must in fact be supervillains. Members include The Chimp, KangaRuby, Nightingale and we're not sure about the slug in the plastic box.'

Up on the roof, the Fish Fingers were quickly regretting their plan to sneak into the bank down the chimney, since the bank didn't seem to have a chimney.

'One of us should have checked,' said Slug Boy, as a burst from a water cannon flew over their heads.

'**We have to split up**,' The Chimp yelled to Nightingale. 'You take off with Slug Boy and try to find out what's going on. Me and KangaRuby will have to take our chances across the rooftops. Meet us at the park.'

Nightingale nodded and soared off into the clouds.

'**Come on, keep moving!**' The Chimp yelled to KangaRuby, grabbing her by the arm. As they dashed for their lives across the roof tiles, they were blasted by every item of weaponry Agent Lemon and his troops could throw. A trail of explosions followed their footsteps until The Chimp and KangaRuby leapt off the bank roof onto the building next door – a cinema – and then over to an office block. But after that there was nowhere else to go. The office block was the last building in the street and it was just too high to jump down.

'We've got to GO BACK the way we came,' yelled The Chimp.

'No, we can make it,' said KangaRuby. 'My legs are springier than yours, grab hold of me.'

'I'm not sure,' said The Chimp. 'That's a long way down and . . .'

Suddenly there was an explosion on the tiles behind them. The Chimp leapt into KangaRuby's arms and she held him like a bridegroom carries a bride. Then she jumped off the edge of the roof, screaming

GERONIMOOOOOOOO!

KangaRuby's super springy legs cushioned their fall and they bounced as if they were on a bungee rope before landing safely. There was a pretty awkward moment at the end because they were kind of, sort of, cuddling and it felt very weird and a bit yucky. The Chimp quickly let go and scrambled to his feet. 'Er. Ahem. Thanks for that. Right, let's leg it!' and they dashed off before the M25 could figure out what had happened. A few minutes later all the Fish Fingers were sitting under a slide in the park and it wasn't long before their superpowers had worn off. They trudged back towards Fish Street.

'Let's go back to mine and wait for Agent Lemon,' said Gary. 'We know we didn't steal Ricky Junior so it must have been The Nuggets. And that means he might be inside Tereza's truck. Come on!'

ONLY THE LONELY

When Gary, Bel, Ruby and Morris burst through the door of Gary's house, Agent Lemon was already there.

Gary rushed over to him. 'Where's Ricky Junior? Did you find him? Was he in *Fnunderbride?*' he demanded.

'I'm really sorry,' said Agent Lemon. 'He's now in the hands of a new gang of villains called the Four Fish Cakes, or something. But rest assured we'll get Rocky home for you one day.'

'MY HAMSTER'S NAME IS RICKY!' Gary shouted. Tears started to stream down his face. His hamster was gone. And it was clear Agent Lemon had absolutely no idea where he was.

Gary's dad put an arm round his son. 'Come on, it'll be all right,' he said.

Gary shook his head. 'No it won't.'

'You can come back to mine if you like and –' said Morris.

'Get lost,' snapped Gary. 'I don't need you and I don't need anybody. I just want to be on my own!'

He'd lost all hope. It was obvious he'd never see his little pet again and he ran out of the back door into his garden and locked himself in the shed.

The others ran after him and Morris tapped on the door. 'Come on, mate,' he said.

Gary didn't answer.

'He'll be all right,' Gary's dad said. 'He just needs some time.'

It was getting chilly now and Agent Lemon zipped up his jacket and headed for the garden gate. 'When you see Gary, tell him we'll track down this new gang real soon,' he said. 'By tomorrow we'll have their horrible faces on Wanted posters plastered all over town, I promise.'

As the secret agent left, Ruby suddenly had an idea. It was just the thing to cheer Gary up. 'Quick! Follow me!' she said to Bel and Morris. 'I know somebody who can help!'

Twenty minutes later, the children were back and they went straight round to the shed. Gary was still sniffing behind the door.

'Mate, it's us,' said Morris.

Choking back his tears, Gary said, 'I thought I told you to take a running jump.'

'Hey, kiddo,' said a voice Gary wasn't expecting. 'If it's running and jumping you need, I'm the guy because I've got world records!'

The shed door burst open. '**Ricky Zigzag!**' shouted Gary, flinging his arms around the superstar.

Ricky chatted to the children in the garden for over an hour. He told Gary he knew exactly what it was like to lose a pet because when he was a boy his kitten had run away from home. 'She came back though, a week later, with mud in her fur and oil on her tail. I think she must have stolen a car and taken it for a test drive!' he laughed. 'So don't give up hope about your hamster.'

Before he left, Gary asked Ricky for his autograph but nobody could find a pen.

'I tell you what,' Ricky said, 'come round to the house tomorrow morning and I'll give you something even better. Something to really cheer you up.' As he walked to the gate, he reminded them, 'And don't forget it's still hush-hush about me being back in Tumchester. I like being left alone by the press for a change. Just until the Trophy Games begin. Only a few more days now!'

After Ricky had gone Gary said, 'That was epic wasn't it?'

'He is sooo nice,' said Bel.

'Even better looking than he is on the posters,' said Ruby.

'Speaking of posters,' said Morris. 'We're going to see our own faces on a few by tomorrow. And they'll have the word Wanted written at the top. So we need to be a bit careful.'

'Why did you have to say that?' asked Gary. 'I was just starting to cheer up a bit. Let's stick to the subject of Ricky Zigzag and how awesome he is. I can't wait to tell Snoddy and Ferret we've seen him again.'

'Whoa, hold it right there, cowboy,' said Morris. 'Don't forget it's still hush-hush.'

'Yeah, for the newspaper and TV people,' said Gary. 'That doesn't mean we can't tell a few people at school.'

'Of course it does!' said Morris. 'Are you nuts?'

'Look, Morris, I'm getting a bit sick of you telling me what to do,' said Gary. 'And that's sick in a bad way, like your stupid Sick Socks.'

'I'm only trying to . . .' said Morris.

'Well don't,' said Gary. 'Just . . . just . . . clear off, will you?'

'All right,' said Morris. 'I will.' And with that, he stormed out of the garden.

Gary went inside and the two girls decided to go home too. They'd try to patch things up in the morning when Gary was feeling a bit more like his usual self.

Meanwhile, deep underground at Wiggy's Bottom, Zultar was talking to his mum on the 4D hologram phone.

'You've done a wonderful job,' said the Great Elder. 'We're very proud of you.'

'Thanks,' said Zultar.

'It was a stroke of genius to double cross the supervillains. With them in prison, we don't have to pay them off and I did enjoy watching it on TV. The signal was remarkably good considering it had to travel forty-seven million-chillion miles.'

'The hamsters are now all loaded onto Flunk's ship,' said Zultar. 'And the two of us will leave Earth in convoy in half an hour. I'm just going to have a bath.'

'Hold on, it's your father here, son,' said Zultar's dad as his hologram appeared. 'You looked after your brother very nicely today. Kept him well out of harm's way. What do you fancy for your tea?'

'How about rock cakes?' said Zultar. 'But don't put real rocks in.'

'Real rocks!' laughed Mr Great Elder. 'You are funny, Zultar.'

'I am, aren't I?' he chuckled. 'It's that Mission-Almost-Accomplished feeling.'

'Well done, son. See you later,' said his dad and ended the call.

Zultar went to find his brother, who was in the

kitchen, filling a bucket with soapy water. Zultar looked in horror but Flunk said, 'Don't worry. I'm not going to drink it. I'm going to wash the spaceships.'

'Great idea,' said Zultar. 'We'll be getting a hero's welcome when we get home so we don't want to arrive with mud on our wing flaps. Here, take the atomic liquidizer because I'm going to have a bath. Keep guard, keep quiet and keep out of trouble. Bring me a towel in about fifteen minutes then it's time for blast off.'

Flunk put the weapon in his back pocket, took the lift and stepped outside. It was getting dark now and the rocks around the hideout cast spooky shadows in the dying light. Flunk got out his bleeper and turned the invisibility shield off. Then he dipped his sponge into the bucket and started to slosh on the suds. After a while he stepped back to see if he'd missed anywhere but he felt something squidgy under his foot. It was another foot. Not one of his own feet either. Somebody else's foot. And the owner of the foot, said, '*Aarggh! Gerroff!*' The foot belonged to Morris.

Morris had been sitting on a rock for the last hour. Ever since Gary had told him to clear off he'd wanted to go to the remotest place he could think of and that was Wiggy's Bottom. He was sitting in the shadows feeling very sorry for himself when he saw

158

the giant alien rise out of the turf. He was expecting to change into Slug Boy but inexplicably nothing had happened. So Morris had watched in petrified silence as the alien washed his spaceship. Then the creature stood on Morris's toe.

'Sorry, little guy. Didn't see you there,' said Flunk. He peered closely at Morris. 'Hey, do I know you? I never forget a face.'

'I-I-I don't think so,' said Morris.

'Funny,' said Flunk. 'It feels like I've seen you before but I'm imagining you smaller somehow. And squidgier.'

'Could be my brother,' fibbed Morris. 'He looks a bit like that.'

Flunk licked his finger and put it in Morris's ear, Morris yelled and Flunk quickly apologised. 'Sorry,' he said. 'It's what we Nrrmmffians do when we meet new people.'

'It just tickled a bit, that's all,' said Morris. He licked his finger and Flunk bent down so Morris could shove it in. 'I'm Morris,' he said.

'I'm Flunk,' said Flunk. 'What you doing up here?'

'I come here to think,' said Morris. 'Normally I sit on a rock over there but it seems to have gone. A few of my favourite sitting-down rocks seem to have vanished.'

'Sorry, that was probably me,' said Flunk. 'I've eaten a few. I have a very healthy appetite.'

'I do too,' admitted Morris. 'But I don't eat rocks. Donuts usually.'

'Back home I get called "fatty" sometimes,' said Flunk.

'Me too,' said Morris. 'But I just have big bones.'

'So do I,' said Flunk.

Morris took out a chocolate donut from his pocket but as he did so, he didn't notice a little matchbox drop out onto the ground. Morris held out the donut to Flunk. 'Do you want half?' he asked.

Flunk beamed, gently took some donut and wolfed it down. 'This is great!' he said. 'We don't have anything this good back home!'

'Where's your home?' asked Morris.

'Planet Nrrmmff. It's up there somewhere,' said Flunk gazing at the stars, trying to pick it out. As he swivelled around searching for it, Morris could see the atomic liquidizer poking from Flunk's back pocket. Morris silently plucked it out and hid it up his jumper.

Still looking at the stars, Flunk turned back. 'Oh, I can never remember which one it is.'

'So why are you here?' asked Morris.

Flunk explained that they'd come to steal hamsters and they were now all on board his spaceship. 'But it's top secret, don't tell anyone.'

'I won't.'

'I thought it was a bad idea. I said to my mum – she's in charge back home – "Why don't we just ask the Earth people nicely?" but my mum said, "Have you seen what they do to each other? They argue and fight all the time. The Earthlings are bound to say no. So if we need hamsters, we're going to have to steal them." Me and my brother were sent to do it and it'll save our whole planet.'

'Save your whole planet?'

'Yep. Everything on Nrrmmff runs on hamster energy. Without it, hospitals will close, all the lights will go out, we won't be able to cook or heat our homes. Everything will stop. We've been running on our energy reserves for weeks because our hamsters all got poorly. Now the reserves are almost gone.'

'How many of you guys live on Nrrmmff?' asked Morris.

'It's a seven with nine zeroes.'

'That's . . . wow,' said Morris. He was sure it was seven billion. 'That's the same number of people on Earth.'

'Is it?' said Flunk. 'Well I never!' He picked up the bucket and squeezed out the sponge. 'I'd better just finish cleaning my spaceship because we're leaving soon. If it's not done, my brother Zultar will tell me off.'

'Zultar is your brother? You don't look very alike,' said Morris.

'I guess we don't,' said Flunk, as the thought occurred to him for the first time. 'Everybody else on Nrrmmff looks quite like Zultar actually. I'm the only one who looks like me. Hey, nice socks by the way.'

'They're called Sick Socks,' said Morris. 'If your tummy's feeling funny you can, you know, chuck up in them.'

'Trendy and useful!' said Flunk. 'I wish I'd had some on yesterday when I ate too many rocks. Do they come in threes?'

'I don't think so,' chuckled Morris. 'Do you win many three-legged races on Nrrmmff?'

'I used to,' said Flunk. 'Until they said it was cheating to have three real legs. I was sad about that because running's my favourite sport.'

'It's a shame you're leaving tonight,' said Morris.

'There's going to be a big sports event called the Trophy Games in a few days. All the best runners in the world are coming to Tumchester. But . . . when I think about it, you might be arrested if you try to get into the stadium.'

Flunk nodded his head. 'Yes, we haven't made many friends on this trip, have we?' He started washing the spaceship again.

Morris thought hard about what to do next. He knew now that Gary's hamster was on board Flunk's spaceship and it was leaving soon. Gary was his protector, his brother in arms and his best friend. Ricky Junior meant the world to him. Morris could use the atomic liquidizer to stop the spaceship. He felt the weapon under his jumper. Yes, that's what he had to do, he had to stand up, aim it like a revolver and pull the trigger. Blast the alien to save the hamsters.

The spaceship was gleaming like a bauble on a Christmas tree. Flunk turned back to Morris and said, 'I'd better get going. My brother will be out of the bath in a minute. Nice meeting you.' As he began to walk away Morris took the weapon from out of his jumper and pointed it at Flunk's back. The muscles in his stomach tightened as he called out, 'Hey, Flunk!'

Flunk turned. Then Morris had a change of heart.

'Er, you dropped this,' he said, handing the weapon over.

'Oh, thanks! I'd have been in B-I-G trouble if I'd lost that,' said Flunk. 'It's an atomic liquidizer. You can use it to blast people. Hey, you'd better hide if you want to see us lift off. It'll be spectacular but Zultar is funny about strangers. I'm not. I always say a stranger's just a friend you haven't met yet.'

'That's nice,' said Morris, smiling.

'On the other hand, my brother says a stranger's a weird bogey man who'll bite your head off and lock you in a dungeon,' added Flunk.

'I prefer yours,' said Morris.

'Me too,' said Flunk.

Morris ducked out of sight as Flunk took the lift that took him down to the hideout and he watched as a few minutes later, the alien emerged again, this time with Zultar at his side.

'I've locked up,' said Zultar to his brother. 'Turned

off the central heating and set the alarm. The co-ordinates for Nrrmmff are all programmed into the spaceships so we should be back in time for tea.'

'Last one home is a Battoloovian frog scab!' joked Flunk, climbing aboard his spaceship. Soon the flying saucers burst into life – Flunk's gave a big roar, Zultar's just a little squeak – and in two flashes of brilliant light, they were gone.

Morris sniffed, put his hands in his pockets and set off home. He had helped save an entire planet but what would Gary do if he ever found out that Morris could have rescued Ricky Junior and didn't? He must never find out.

CLUES IN THE NEWS

The next morning a woman who was walking her dog on Wiggy's Bottom discovered a patch of burnt grass where the spaceships had taken off. She also found a mysterious bucket of soapy water and a sponge. The woman knew it was odd so she called the police, who quickly turned the area into a crime scene. Detective Rigley called Agent Lemon and they both arrived and went over the area with a fine toothcomb. Detective Rigley actually used a fine-tooth toothbrush because he had lost his comb.

A press conference was held and Agent Lemon revealed more clues of what must have happened when the aliens made their getaway. 'Good morning,' he said. 'I'm from the M25. Not the motorway, the other one. Actually, I probably shouldn't have mentioned that because we're a top-secret organisation and now I'm going to have to arrest you all. Unless you promise not to tell anyone.'

They all did.

'Okay,' Agent Lemon continued. 'This was clearly

the launch site for the alien spaceships. The burns on the grass suggest they took off at approximately seventeen times the speed of light. That's really fast. The bucket's made of no earthly substance – it's lighter than tissue paper and stronger than steel. The sponge is also of alien origin. It's the spongiest sponge known to man and spongier than a really spongy sponge cake. Cosmic dust on the ground and three large footprints confirm a non-human presence. We conclude the big furry alien was here. We also found some teeny-tiny footprints, which must have belonged to that nuggety alien. It seems we didn't destroy him at the bank after all.'

The reporters busily wrote everything down.

'Now, we did find some other stuff which leads us to believe the aliens had help – human help. That's a police matter so over to you, Detective Rigley.'

Detective Rigley picked up the microphone. It made a horrible **squealing** noise and he said, '**1, 2, 1, 2, testing, testing**.' The reporters wrote that down, which was a bit silly really. When the squealing stopped the policeman carried on. 'First, we discovered a set of footprints size four, from not very trendy boy's trainers. Next, we found crumbs from a chocolate donut, with traces of both human and non-human saliva, indicating that the donut was shared with an alien. Finally, we found this matchbox with the word 'Beware' written on it. Put these clues together and we think somebody out there can give us a name.'

Gary had been watching the news on his bedroom telly. Donuts? Not very trendy trainers? A matchbox with 'Beware' written on it? Gary could give them a name all right but he didn't want to believe it. Why would Morris share a donut with an alien? What had really happened at Wiggy's Bottom? Gary got on his bike and pedalled as fast as he could to Morris's house. When he got there, Ruby and Bel were just arriving too. They'd seen the same news conference and had come up with the same name. Gary rang the doorbell and Morris's mum answered it.

'Wipe your feet,' she said. 'He's upstairs.' Gary, Ruby and Bel sprinted up to Morris's bedroom and found him sitting on a chair, his head in his hands. He'd seen the news conference too.

Gary tried to stay calm. 'Last night, you saw the aliens, didn't you?'

'Yes,' said Morris.

'So what happened? Did you really help them?'

'It's a long story,' said Morris, already with tears in his eyes. 'I met one of the aliens. The one with the three legs, the horns and the spikes – Flunk.'

'Did he try to kidnap you and stick you in his

spaceship?' asked Ruby.

'No,' said Morris. 'We chatted for a bit and shared a donut. Then I stole his atomic liquidizer, the spoon thing.'

'So why didn't you use it?' asked Bel.

'I don't know. I ended up giving it back to him,' said Morris.

'You . . . helped him escape? You let him take Ricky Junior?' said Gary, his voice rising.

'Yes,' said Morris.

Gary's face turned the colour of beetroot. He gritted his teeth and a lump came to his throat. The breath wouldn't come.

'Why, Morris?' asked Ruby.

'Because everybody on Planet Nrrmmff would die without those hamsters,' said Morris. 'And do you know how many lives that is? Seven and nine zeroes.'

'But they're alien lives,' said Bel. 'They're horrible creatures that look like chicken nuggets or giant sabre-toothed monsters.'

'Does it matter what they look like?' said Morris. 'That's racism!'

'It doesn't matter what they look like but it matters what they do,' said Bel.

Gary's head was still swimming but he could speak his mind now. 'And they stole pets from the hands of kids. And one of those kids was your best friend. Me,' said Gary.

'I thought I was doing the right thing,' said Morris.

'Well, you thought wrong!' yelled Gary.

'You didn't even try to save Ricky, did you?' said Ruby.

'No,' said Morris.

'Did you ask your new best friend, this Flunk, about Ricky Junior at all?' asked Bel.

'No.'

'Then you let us all down. Especially Gary,' said Bel.

Ruby couldn't look Morris in the eyes. She just shook her head.

Morris tried one last time. 'The hamsters will get used to their new lives and all the children in Tumchester will get new pets and . . .'

'Superheroes are supposed to fight supervillains,' said Gary. 'Not share donuts with them. We're finished as mates, finished.'

'I don't know what to say,' said Morris. 'I'm . . . sorry.'

The others walked out of Morris's bedroom and left him sitting on the bed. He buried his face in his pillow and soon it was wet with tears.

YOU NEVER CAN TELL

The next morning, Gary woke up and – as he always did – glanced over to check that his hamster was okay. Of course, the cage wasn't there and Gary's mind churned with memories of the last few days. He put the duvet back over his head until his dad walked in with a bowl of cornflakes. 'Rise and shine, son,' he said, opening the curtains.

As the sun streaked in Gary remembered the only good thing that had happened in the last week. He told his dad to tell Ruby and Bel that he'd see them at school and he set off for Grimley Avenue. As he walked along the road, he could see Wanted posters for the Four Fish Fingers on every billboard, every tree and every lamppost. It made him jumpy but it also made him think of Morris. 'No way am I going to be in the Fish Fingers with him,' he said to himself.

When he rang the doorbell of number 60 an upstairs curtain drew back for a second and then Gary heard footsteps on the stairs.

'Hi, kiddo, you're right on time,' said Ricky,

opening the door just a little. He checked that there was nobody else about and said, 'Wait there, I've got something brilliant for you.'

He returned with a felt tip and a gold silky running vest. 'What shall I write on it?'

'**Epic!**' said Gary. 'If you could write *"To Gary, Bel, Ruby and er . . . Ruby's gran".*'

'Sure,' said Ricky. 'But what about the chubby guy? Morris, isn't it?'

'We've fallen out,' admitted Gary. 'He did something really mean. He could have saved my hamster's life but he didn't.'

'Okay,' said Ricky, 'If you're sure,' and he signed the vest just the way Gary asked him to.

'**Wow–wow–wow–wow!**' said Gary. '**Thanks so so so much**.'

'And how about a little training session after school?' suggested Ricky. 'Come back about four with your mates and bring Ruby's gran. Now *she* had talent!'

It was just what Gary needed to take his mind off Morris and his hamster. 'Awesome, sick, thanks very much!' he said and rushed off to school.

At break time Gary sat on a bench by the school field with Ruby and Bel. It was the first chance he'd had to tell them about Ricky's running vest and he carefully got it out of his bag, making sure nobody else was around to see it.

'**Woweee!**' said Ruby.

'It's . . . beautiful,' said Bel.

'Totally sick, isn't it?' said Gary.

Just then Morris came out to the playground and he spotted the others on the bench. He decided he'd try to make up with them but when he got closer, he noticed the vest and the autographs written across it. When he saw his name wasn't on it, he bit his lip and headed for another bench. Gary put the vest back in his bag.

'It's his own fault,' he said to the girls.

Gary was just about to go off and find a game of football to join when Snoddy and Ferret sidled over.

'How come Doris is sitting on his own then?' asked Snoddy.

'It's none of your business,' said Gary.

'Have you two had a tiff?' said Snoddy. 'What a shame. I wonder why? Wouldn't he let you borrow his Sick Socks?'

Ferret sniggered. 'Hey, what's in the bag? Is it another cardie for Ruby in case she gets cold? Or do they get delivered by her gran in her slippers? **HEH HEH HEH**.'

Ruby shook her head but Gary had had enough. 'I'll show you what it is,' he said, unzipping his bag and pulling out the vest. 'It's something I got from

173

Ricky Zigzag this morning but you can't say anything.'

Snoddy snatched it and looked at the autographs. It was clearly the real thing. The two bullies were lost for words.

'I told you he was living on Grimley Avenue,' said Gary.

'But like Gary told you, it's a secret,' said Ruby. 'So you can't tell anyone.'

'Right, yeah, okay,' said Snoddy and Ferret and they headed off.

That night, straight after school, Gary, Ruby and Bel dashed home to change, then zoomed off again to Grimley Avenue with Ruby's gran. She wasn't wearing her slippers this time. She had proper trainers on.

Ricky was enjoying his life away from the spotlight and his training was going well. 'I've got a feeling I might just break a world record at the games!' he told them. 'So long as there are no distractions between now and then.' There was a lot more space in the back garden than the children had imagined and Ricky got them to do some stretches and a few warm-up sprints. Then he laid out some little hurdles. 'These are perfect for beginners,' he said.

One at a time, the three children (and one old age pensioner) ran and jumped and fell over and giggled until their sides were ready to burst. Ricky gave them lots of tips, teaching them to pump their arms up and down, and showing them how to leap the hurdles without having to stop.

Just then the doorbell rang and Ricky went to answer it. He came back a few minutes later, frowning and shaking his head. 'Sorry, kiddos,' he said. 'Practice is over. The press are outside. My secret's out, some rat must have blabbed.'

'**AWWWW**,' said Ruby and Bel.

'What a shame,' said Ruby's gran.

Gary didn't say anything. His face told its own story. Ricky looked at him quizzically. 'Are you all right, Gary?' he asked.

Gary didn't answer. He just looked at the floor.

'You didn't have anything to do with this, did you?' asked Ricky.

'I . . . think . . . yes, I might have done,' said Gary. 'I . . . I . . . there are some boys at school — Snoddy and Ferret — and I . . . told them. They were winding me up and . . . I . . . I'm really sorry.'

'Well, thanks very much. I've got a press conference to do now,' said Ricky. 'Then I'll have to pack my bags because I can't stay here any more.' He shook Ruby's gran by the hand and gave the girls a hug. Then he walked to the door, still shaking his head. 'It was great to meet you, kids. At least, some of you.'

Outside, the front garden was full of reporters, TV cameras and autograph hunters jostling for space on the lawn like penguins at a pilchard party. The flashbulbs popped as Ricky opened the door and stood on the step. Gary, Bel, Ruby and her gran left by the patio at the back and quickly pushed their way through the crowds where they bumped into Snoddy. He was there with his dog Belcher and his dad, who was looking very smug.

'Hey, thanks for the tip-off, Gaz,' said Snoddy. 'I told my dad about Ricky so he rang his mate on the *Tumchester Times* and we've made a ton of cash! My dad's gonna buy me a new skateboard now, ain't ya, Dad?'

'It's the least I can do, son,' sniggered Snoddy's dad.

Gary wanted to knock Snoddy's head off. '**It was supposed to be a secret!**' he yelled.

'Oh, yeah, sorry, I forgot,' said Snoddy.

Gary clenched his fists but before he exploded, Ruby's gran pulled him away.

'We'll have no fisticuffs here,' she said.

Ricky started to speak to the reporters. He was smiling but he didn't sound very happy. 'Yes, you've caught me,' he said. 'As you can see, my training base in the Peruvian mountains is actually a little semi-detached house in Tumchester but it's been great to lie low for a while. I'll be joining the other athletes at the team camp tomorrow.'

As Gary, Bel, Ruby and Ruby's gran walked home, Gary kept saying, 'It's all my fault, it's all my fault. I'm the rat who blabbed.' And nobody said it wasn't.

DO THE RIGHT THING

The next day, Gary woke up early as usual. It had been a sleepless night and as he plodded downstairs for his breakfast his head churned. He had lost his hamster, he had lost his best mate and the superstar he idolised thought he was a rat.

He walked into the kitchen where his dad was reading the paper. The front-page headline was *Ricky Runs Into Trouble* and there was a big picture of him surrounded by reporters on Grimley Avenue.

'Mornin',' said Gary's dad.

Gary just sniffed.

'Hey, there's a letter for you,' said his dad, handing Gary an envelope.

Gary took it and saw Ricky Zigzag's name printed on the back in gold lettering. Gary didn't want to open it. He thought Ricky might be writing to tell him off but his dad said, 'Go on, read it. It's the least you can do since you dropped him in it.'

Gary flipped open the envelope and found tickets inside to the opening ceremony of the Trophy

Games. There was a letter too and as Gary read it, his whole universe changed.

The letter said:

Hi, kiddo, I was gutted last night, I can't say I wasn't. You made me a promise and you broke it. But you admitted your mistake and apologised and that was cool of you. So forget it. Me and you, we're mates and always will be. Share the tickets with your pals. Even that chubby kid Morris. Maybe it's time to forgive and forget with him now? And if you look on your front step you'll find a package. See you at the Games!

Ricky Z

Gary couldn't believe it. Tears rolled down his cheeks. '**Awesome! Epic! Epic awesome!**' he yelled, running to the front door. He found the parcel on the step and pulled off the wrapping paper. Inside was another running vest but this time the message was:

To Morris, Look after your mates. They're the family you choose for yourself,

All the best,
Ricky Z

Gary didn't bother to change out of his pyjamas. He shoved on some trainers, hopped on his bike and pedalled as fast as he could to Morris's house. When he knocked on Morris's front door, Morris's mum said he wasn't in. 'He told me he was going to school early today.'

Gary knew Morris would never do that and he guessed where he'd be. Somewhere out of the way, having a think. He went to collect Ruby and Bel and half an hour later, they arrived at Wiggy's Bottom where they found Morris alone on a rock.

'Y'alright?' said Gary.

'Suppose so,' said Morris. 'Why are you wearing your pyjamas?'

'It's a long story,' said Gary. He sat down next to Morris. 'Look, mate,' he said. 'I'm really, really sorry I lost my nut. I was disappointed, you know, with what you did because I loved that little hamster. But I know you had your reasons.'

Morris swallowed hard. There was a little lump in his throat that wouldn't go away. 'Flunk, the alien, said the hamsters would be really well looked after and that was a big reason. But the main thing was, if I'd stopped that spaceship, a whole planet would have been wiped out. Do you know how many lives that would have been? Seven billion. And do you know how many people there are on Planet Earth?'

'Seven billion,' gasped Bel. 'It's exactly the same.'

'I'm really sorry I let you down,' said Morris. 'But I still think I made the right choice. I did it even though I knew Gary might not forgive me and I might lose you all as my friends, and that means more to me than anything.'

'It's okay,' said Gary. 'You did a really brave thing. You did the *right* thing. And I was a rubbish best mate.'

'We were all rubbish mates,' added Ruby.

'We're very sorry, Morris,' said Bel.

Gary put his hand up for knuckles and Morris gave him knuckles back. It was the first time in his life Morris had done it perfectly. Then Gary gave his best friend the gift from Ricky Zigzag. Morris couldn't believe it. He put it on over his jumper and just kept smiling.

'Suppose we'd better get to school!' said Bel.

'I'd better change out of my pyjamas first,' said Gary. 'Snoddy would never let me forget it otherwise!' Then they leapt back on their bikes and rode off down the hill.

LET THE GAMES BEGIN

A few days later, at the opening ceremony for the Trophy Games Gary, Ruby, Bel and Morris were sitting in VIP seats right next to the track. Ricky had arranged for a posh car to pick them up and after a short drive along streets festooned with bunting they were escorted to their seats by smartly dressed stewards. The atmosphere in the stadium fizzed with excitement. So many people, so many colours, so much noise. The only disturbing thing for the Fish Fingers were the Wanted posters with their faces on up on the walls.

'It's a good job we've got secret identities,' said Bel.

They tried to put it out of their minds.

The opening ceremony began with fireworks and then troops of dancers gambolled around the running track and across the pitch, dressed in costumes to represent Tumchester through the ages, everything from furry cavemen skins to sparkly astronauts. Then gymnasts came out to create a human version of Tumchester Bridge and finally, a giant Sick Sock was brought out and the man on the loud speakers said, 'Let's have a big round of applause for the world's most famous sock. It was invented by Tumchester's own Dr Nobby Diddle almost ten years ago.' The jingle from the TV advert played, *Before you take them to the Doc's, put them in our socks!* and the giant Sick Sock (with four dancers inside) wriggled across the pitch to cheers from around the stadium.

The ceremony came to a climax when the athletes entered the stadium. Each team was led by a smart steward with a flag and after a walk around the running track they all came to stand in the middle of the arena. Ricky Zigzag spotted the children and gave them a wave. Then there was a laser show and suddenly a huge spaceship descended from the clouds and hovered over the stadium.

'That's well cool,' said Gary. 'The best bit of the show so far.'

'Like something out of Hollywood,' said Bel.

'Crikey on a bikey,' said Ruby. 'It's the size of a hotel!'

Morris just said, '**ER . . . ER . . .**' because the shape

seemed strangely familiar. Just like the one that Flunk had soared off in. Only bigger. Much, much bigger.

There was a fanfare of trumpets and suddenly a huge 4D hologram appeared of a chicken nugget with a long beard. 'Don't be alarmed,' said the hologram of the Great Elder. 'We come in peace. I'm speaking to you now, live by satellite from Planet Nrrmmff. We borrowed some of your hamsters for a few days without asking. I'm very sorry and I've sent this spaceship to return them.'

The emotions of the crowd went from astonishment to fear to anger to forgiveness to joy. The hamsters were coming home! There was a huge cheer as an enormous ramp descended from the spaceship and row upon row of chicken-nugget sized aliens in tight trousers marched down. They had shiny spoons strapped to their backs and each one was carrying a hamster in a cage. There was even a name and address label on the front of them. It certainly was a spectacular sight.

In the cockpit of the spaceship, Flunk sat next to Zultar. 'This is brilliant, isn't it?' he said. 'Look at all their little human faces. And their little hamster faces. I wish I could be the one telling them.'

Zultar smiled.

The Great Elder carried on. 'The hamsters have all been well looked after. We just needed them to give our energy supplies a little top-up. Your brave pets have saved over seven billion lives.'

Another huge cheer.

'Their cages are all fitted with a homing device and on my signal, they'll fly automatically to their homes.'

The Nrrmmffian hamster carriers now stood around the centre of the arena in formation. The athletes were still standing on the grass in the middle and the audience were clapping and cheering. Gary was jumping up and down with joy. 'I'm going to see Ricky Junior again! That's amazing!'

'Okay, release them!' the Great Elder said, and the cages fluttered off into the pale blue sky as if they had butterfly wings.

In the cockpit, Flunk beamed. His mum was so brilliant she made him really proud sometimes. Then suddenly there were flashes of blinding light, another fanfare and the stadium was engulfed in smoke. As the smoke cleared, the atmosphere seemed to have changed. The Nrrmmffians were now pointing their spoons at the athletes in a slightly threatening way.

Something else had happened too. Gary, Morris, Ruby and Bel had transformed into the Fabulous Four Fish Fingers. Worried about being recognised from their Wanted posters, the superheroes dashed towards the only place they could see to hide –

inside the giant Sick Sock. The dancers had left it
lying on the ground and luckily everyone was still
too busy looking at the huge hologram to notice.
Huddling inside the sock, the Fish Fingers were still
quite baffled. Why had they transformed? It didn't
take long for their question to get a terrible answer.

'Hi, everyone, back to me again,' the Great Elder
said. 'You know when I said we come in peace, I was
lying. We don't. I'm the destroyer of dark matter. And
light matter. To be honest, all matter. Even matter that
doesn't matter. We've decided that hamsters aren't
the way to go any more. They're a bit small
and the future's going to be different.
We've decided we need some bigger
animals. Animals that are in peak
physical condition. Animals
that'll run all day. In short,
human athletes!'

The crowd sat in their seats in stunned silence. Nothing seemed real. The big alien was joking, wasn't she? They started to boo and hiss.

'It's not a pantomime,' said the Great Elder. 'We're deadly serious.' She pointed her finger at the Nrrmmffian troops, who started blasting random things to prove how serious they were. They zapped a hot dog stand, a floodlight and a flagpole, turning them all into smouldering, melted blobs of goo. The crowd gasped.

In the spaceship cockpit, Flunk and Zultar were watching through the windscreen. Zultar was chuckling but Flunk was very confused. His mum had told him they were only going back to Earth to deliver the hamsters. He'd stuck the address labels on the cages himself. 'Mum never said anything about stealing humans,' he said to his brother.

'But that's why the ship's cargo bay is full of big cages with the wheels inside,' said Zultar. 'Don't worry, the humans will love it.'

'They don't seem very happy now,' said Flunk, looking at the faces of the athletes in the stadium.

'It was actually you who put the idea in my head,' said Zultar. 'And I told Mum.'

'I don't understand,' said Flunk.

'On the night we left Earth you told me it was

a shame we were leaving just before the Trophy Games,' said Zultar. 'You told me they'd be the greatest sporting occasion Tumchester had ever seen. And that's when I thought of using human runners instead of hamsters. Mum loved it!'

Flunk was devastated. He ate a hat he'd brought in case his ear got cold just to take his mind off things.

The Nrrmmffian troops started blasting the ground by the athletes' feet and they had no choice but to start walking. Ricky Zigzag tried to dash off in the other direction but he was spotted by a Nrrmmffian who set his atomic liquidizer to *JELLY (LEGS)* and fired a beam at him. Ricky ran quickly, using all his hurdling skill, dodging, weaving, leaping, trying to jink out of the way but the beam hit Ricky in the knee. He felt the bones in his legs turn to jelly and he wibbled and wobbled back to the other athletes. They were marching up the ramp to the spaceship, shouting and screaming, and the crowd were yelling too.

In the cockpit, Flunk said, 'I don't like it. I don't like it one bitty bit.'

'Listen to me,' said Zultar sternly. 'You need to wake up and smell the Giant Sliverian weasel milkshake. We're just borrowing a few silly people from a useless world to solve the energy problems of a much better planet – ours! It doesn't matter if the Earthlings don't like it.'

'I don't like it,' said Flunk.

'What you're saying is treachery,' said Zultar. 'Do you think you're cleverer than the Great Elder herself? You need to be careful, Flunk, or you might find yourself in jail.'

Inside the giant Sick Sock, the Fish Fingers tried to figure out a plan.

'**Macbeth!**' Nightingale suddenly said.

'Come again?' said Slug Boy.

'It's Shakespeare,' said Nightingale. 'We did it at school. In *Macbeth*, soldiers disguise themselves as a forest and slowly creep up to a castle. Nobody notices. We need to do the same!'

'But we're disguised as an

enormous hi-visibility Sick Sock, not a forest!' said Slug Boy. 'I think the nuggets might spot us!'

'Not if we move slowly,' said Nightingale.

'We haven't got much time!' said KangaRuby, who'd poked a hole through the sock to see what was happening. 'I think the aliens are about to close the door.'

KangaRuby was right. The last of the athletes were almost at the top of the ramp but at that moment, the superheroes got the break they needed. An M25 helicopter swooped over the sports pitch with Agent Lemon at the controls. He fired at the hologram of the Great Elder and hit the spaceship with a small explosion. It didn't leave a scratch but it did catch everybody's attention. A platoon of nuggets on the ground fired back with their atomic liquidizers as Agent Lemon's helicopter dodged quickly out of the way.

'Close the door,' shouted the Great Elder to the nuggets on the ramp and within seconds, the exits were sealed and the spaceship had blasted off.

Zultar came down from the cockpit to greet the athletes. 'Welcome aboard,' he said. 'We'll be arriving in Nrrmmff in an hour or two. The emergency exits are . . . sorry there aren't any for you lot. And there's no duty-free shopping either. But you do get an in-flight meal.' He took a carrot from his pocket and threw it into the crowd. 'Share it nicely now. You're going to be locked in the cargo bay, where you'll each have your own cage and a wheel to run around on. Take them down, lads,' he instructed.

As the Nrrmmffian guards set off, Zultar turned to go back to the cockpit but he tripped over something on the floor.

'What's this giant sock doing here?' he yelled, stumbling to his feet.

'It's not mine,' said a guard.

'Nor mine,' said another. 'Too big for me and it's definitely not my colour.'

Zultar stuck his atomic liquidizer inside and peered in. Empty. 'One of the athletes must have brought it,' he said. 'I'll get Flunk to take it to a charity shop when we get to Nrrmmff.'

Hiding in the shadows behind a statue of the Great Elder, the Fish Fingers breathed again.

?

'What now?' whispered The Chimp.

'First we need to release the athletes,' said Nightingale.

'Then take over the spaceship,' said KangaRuby.

'And then simply fly it back to Earth?' asked Slug Boy. 'I think I may have spotted a flaw in the plan. None of us knows how to fly an alien spaceship! In fact, we haven't even passed our cycling proficiency tests!'

'I've passed mine,' said The Chimp. 'I did it when you were off with tonsillitis.'

'And we've both got ours,' said KangaRuby and Nightingale together.

'Apologies,' said Slug Boy. 'But just because you can all pedal around a few cones in the playground, doesn't mean you can pilot a flying saucer!'

The others realised Slug Boy had a point. But they decided they would worry about that later. First they had to try to find the athletes. The Fish Fingers crept along the corridor searching for a lift to take them down to the hold.

At that moment, Flunk was doing an inspection of the prisoners. Zultar had ordered him to because he said he was tired of looking at Flunk's grumpy face. Flunk decided not to do any inspecting. Instead he took in a big plate of sandwiches and some cups of coffee but he soon found there wasn't quite enough to go round. He'd only brought six sandwiches and four cups and there were 897 athletes.

'Sorry,' he said and started stirring the coffees with his trousers.

As he handed a cup to Ricky Zigzag he said, 'Hey, would you mind if I had a little go on your runny-roundy wheel?'

Ricky said he didn't mind at all so Flunk got inside and started running on the wheel. He found it was the most fun he had ever, ever, ever had in his life.

Suddenly a voice barked over the ship's intercom.

'Cockpit to cargo bay. Cockpit to cargo bay.' It was Zultar. Flunk panicked and fell off the wheel. He staggered to his feet and stuttered, 'Er, yes, yes, Flunk here. Just finishing the inspection.'

'Well, hurry up,' said Zultar. 'Mum's on the phone.'

'Okay,' said Flunk. 'Just coming.' He thanked Ricky for letting him play and stepped out of the cage, being careful to lock it behind him.

Upstairs, the Fish Fingers had found a big sign that read 'Lift to the Cargo Bay' and soon they were down below, tiptoeing along another brightly lit corridor. They turned a corner and saw Flunk coming out of a door and stopping to speak to two guards. The Fish Fingers stepped back but they heard him say, 'Don't be nasty to them.' The guards nodded but as Flunk walked off they sniggered, winking their one eyes at each other.

Sometimes it takes a moment of individual bravery to change the course of a battle. And on this day, at this time, it was KangaRuby's moment. While the others were whispering about what to do next she walked confidently down the corridor and said to the two guards, 'Excuse me, is the ladies' lavatory down here?'

The guards were so confused by the question, it gave KangaRuby the chance she needed.

'Beg your par–' said one but before he could finish his sentence, KangaRuby put her hand in her pocket. Not the magic pocket in her cardigan, her trouser pocket. She whipped out the giraffe fridge magnet she'd won on Bring Your Pet to Class Day and held it up. Instantly, the nuggets saw their atomic liquidizers fly through the air and KangaRuby caught them both in one hand. The nuggets scarpered as quickly as they could.

The other Fish Fingers were amazed.

'Er, can I just say **WOW!**' said Nightingale, giving her best friend a hug.

'I always said you were an attractive girl!' said Slug Boy. 'Magnets, attractive! Get it?'

KangaRuby gave Slug Boy a **DONK** on the head with the back of an atomic liquidizer and they all laughed.

'How did you know a magnet would work?' asked The Chimp.

'I just guessed,' said KangaRuby, blushing. 'I'm not as green as I am cabbage-looking, as my gran would say.' The others didn't have a clue what that meant, though in truth neither did KangaRuby nor her gran.

'Right, those guards are probably off raising the alarm. We haven't got much time,' said The Chimp. 'Follow me.'

He opened the door to the cargo bay and they nipped inside but they weren't prepared for the horrific scene that greeted them. Cage upon cage of human hamsters. Some of the athletes were trying to sleep on beds of straw, others were sitting sobbing, a few were running on the giant wheels just to keep busy. Ricky Zigzag was trying to prise open the bars of his cage but the metal just wouldn't budge.

'Can I have your attention?' shouted The Chimp. The athletes looked up.

'It's that gang of supervillains!' said a long-distance runner. 'They nicked that kid's hamster from the bank.'

'I had a feeling they were behind it all!' said a high jumper. 'You despicable worms!'

'No, no,' shouted Nightingale. 'You've got it all wrong. We're here to help. We didn't steal any hamsters. In fact, The Chimp had his own pet hamster stolen by the crooks.'

The athletes looked at The Chimp's face and even though he was wearing his mask, they could see the sadness in his eyes. 'It's true, honest,' he said.

'I'm about to sing,' Nightingale carried on.

'There's no time for karaoke,' said a shot putter. 'I thought you were going to rescue us, not audition for *Nrrmmff's Got Talent.*'

Nightingale ignored the remark. 'I'm hoping that my voice will bend the metal in the cages and you can get out,' she said. 'Please put your fingers in your ears.'

The athletes did as she told them and the Fish Fingers did too. Nightingale cleared her throat and started to sing, 'HEY DIDDLE DIDDLE, THE CAT AND THE FIDDLE, THE COW . . .'

Sure enough, the room began to shake, the cages

began to rumble and the sound was deafening but Nightingale carried on. '...JUMPED OVER THE MOON...'

Her voice made the whole ship shudder and when she'd finished most of the cages had crashed onto the floor, their doors hanging open.

The athletes cheered and dashed out of their cages.

'Right,' said The Chimp, 'the next thing we need to do is . . .'

instructed Zultar, who was now standing in the doorway with an angry frown on his face and waving his atomic liquidizer. There were another fifty Nrrmmffian troops standing behind him, weapons loaded, aimed at the athletes and the Fish Fingers.

'Tidy up the cages **NOW**,' said Zultar. 'And then you can all climb back inside. Did you honestly think you could make that racket and I wouldn't hear you? Earthling fools! As for you, Fish Fingers, I have a cabin you can have all to yourselves that I'm sure you'll find most uncomfortable. Guards, lock them in the dirty laundry cupboard under the stairs. And I'll take those atomic liquidizers off you too.' He snatched them out of KangaRuby's hand.

A short time later, the Fish Fingers found themselves in a cramped room where the only light was from a tiny keyhole, roughly the size of Rice Krispie. The Chimp found that his head bumped the ceiling when he stood up and when he stretched out his arms his fingers touched the walls. Underneath their feet was a mountain of small, tight-fitting trousers that needed a wash.

'Whiffy,' gasped Slug Boy.

'Look on the bright side,' said KangaRuby. 'At least we aren't trapped in here with the Bog Snorkeler's laundry. Now that would be stinky.'

They all agreed about that.

'I think I might have another bright side for you to look on,' said Slug Boy, slithering out of the Slug Mobile. 'I reckon I may just be able to squeeze out through that keyhole.'

PILOT LIGHT

Up in the cockpit, Zultar was sipping an iced coffee and checking the instrument panel. Flunk was eating a box of popcorn so fast that he was in danger of swallowing his own fingers.

'Just another hour and we'll be home again,' said Zultar to his brother. 'There'll be medals in this for us.'

'**UMM**,' said Flunk, who was now crunching his way through the empty cardboard box.

Unseen by the aliens, a little black shape slithered under the door. Slug Boy wasn't used to travelling quite so far under his own steam and he was breathing heavily. He promised himself that if he ever got back to Earth he would cut down on donuts and take up aerobics. Or jogging. Or tiddlywinks. Probably tiddlywinks.

He wriggled up the nearest wall and looked around, desperately trying to think of an idea. Could he slither onto a button that reprogrammed the navigation system and turn the ship around? Impossible. He'd need a university degree in rocket science. Nrrmmffian rocket science. How about if he jammed up the ship's computer by slithering inside and splashing his mucus around? No, too dangerous because he might just fry himself. Then he spotted what he needed: Zultar's atomic liquidizer, leaning against a cupboard door. It had been in his hands once before but this time things would be different. For a start, this time he didn't have any hands. And apart from that, this time he was prepared to use it.

'What else can I eat?' Flunk asked his brother. He had devoured every bit of the popcorn box but he was still hungry. 'I worked up quite an appetite on that wheel.'

'**Wheel?**' asked Zultar.

Flunk suddenly remembered that he should have been inspecting the prisoners instead of running around on that runny-roundy wheel.

'Did you say wheel?' Zultar asked again.

'No, not wheel' answered Flunk. 'I said . . . **eel!** Yes, I worked up an appetite wrestling an eel and it was good exercise, but boy has it made me hungry.'

'Wrestling an eel?' said Zultar shaking his head. It was just the sort of barmy thing his brother would do. Zultar didn't want to know where the eel had come from or where it was now. 'Can't you just do something sensible?'

'Why don't **YOU** do something sensible?' said Slug Boy, who was holding Zultar's atomic liquidizer in his mouth and pointing it at him.

'What the?' gasped Zultar.

'Hey, it's that sluggy guy!' said Flunk. 'But I can't quite make out what he's saying.'

With the atomic liquidizer in his mouth Slug Boy couldn't form his words properly. So what Slug Boy said actually sounded like, '**WHAAA DON YEEUGHH DOO SOMINKSESSIL?**'

Slug Boy tried again but this time it came out as, '**WHIRL DON YUUU DOOBY SOM SECIL?**'

'I think he's trying to tell us about a man called Cecil,' said Flunk. 'If it's the Cecil I know, he sells used flying saucers in the shopping centre by our house. I wonder how he knows Cecil. Are you trying to tell us about Cecil?'

Slug Boy shook his head. Then he had an idea. He flicked the atomic liquidizer up into the air and caught it between his eyeballs, curling one tentacle round the top and gripping the trigger with the other. It was really effective and he wondered why he'd never thought of using his eye tentacles like this before. 'I said, Why don't you do something sensible?'

'Like what?' asked Zultar.

'Like turn this ship around?' replied Slug Boy. 'Otherwise, nugget features, I'm going to turn you into a very **Unhappy Meal!**'

'You wouldn't dare,' said Zultar.

'Wouldn't I?' answered Slug Boy, 'Watch me.' He squeezed the trigger of the atomic liquidizer and the beam burned a big hole in the door behind Zultar, who'd ducked just in time.

'Be careful with that thing!' yelled Zultar. 'You'll get us all killed!'

'So if you want to stay alive, **TURN THIS SHIP AROUND NOW!**'

'Shan't,' said Zultar.

'I think the little slug means it,' said Flunk.

'I do mean it,' said Slug Boy, curling his tentacle round the trigger again. 'And don't give me any codswallop about destroying a whole planet. I've heard it all before.'

Zultar sighed and started to reprogram the satnav. 'Right, that's the coordinates set for your pathetic planet. What are you going to do now?'

'Just sit back and enjoy the ride,' said Slug Boy.

Then he noticed Flunk was staring at him really closely.

'Have we met before?' Flunk asked. 'You remind me of somebody, that's all.'

'Obviously we've met before,' said Slug Boy. 'I'm one of the Fabulous Four Fish Fingers. And while I think about it, you can go and get my friends from the laundry room. Do it quickly or my eyeball might just slip on the trigger and bake your brother's brains.'

Flunk headed off and came back a few minutes later with the other Fish Fingers. They congratulated Slug Boy, who seemed completely in control of the situation. At least he was until he suddenly started to wobble, twitch and jerk, his sluggy skin fizzing and he made a kind of **GRUUUUNTING** noise. The Chimp, Nightingale and KangaRuby were transforming too. Their hour of superhero power was up and seconds later they were back to normal.

The atomic liquidizer that Slug Boy had been gripping in his eye tentacle was now lying on the floor and there was a desperate scramble to pick it up. Morris got his fingers round it first, Zultar sank his teeth into Morris's thumb, Flunk picked up both Morris and Zultar in his huge paw, Morris dropped the atomic liquidizer again, Ruby had it, she threw it to Gary, he tossed it towards Bel but Flunk caught it first.

'Well done, brother,' said Zultar. 'That was all a

bit freaky but it's over now. I'll just reprogram the satnav. Again! Then you can give me that atomic . . .'

'Not so fast,' said Flunk, pointing the atomic liquidizer at Zultar. 'I know this chubby kid and he's my friend.'

'Hello again, big fella,' said Morris. 'Lovely to see you.'

'I got some thinking to do,' said Flunk.

'Yes, you do,' said Morris. 'You're holding a very powerful weapon in your hands but do you know what's even more powerful than that?'

'Is it the stink from that Bog Snorkeler guy?' asked Flunk.

'Yes, but that's not what I was thinking of,' said Morris. 'It's the power of words. And I want you to listen to mine now. Flunk, do the right thing. Zultar and your mum are wrong. Hamsters love going round on their wheels. But people don't. And the people you've got locked up downstairs need to go back to their families.'

'Don't listen to him!' Zultar screamed at his brother. 'If you do what he says you'll be chucking your own planet into the dustbin of history. Not the recycling dustbin of history either. There'll be no coming back for any of us. It'll be all over!'

Not for the first time in his life, Flunk looked confused. Then he said to Morris, 'Can I borrow one of your socks?'

Morris looked down and realised he was wearing his Sick Socks. 'Er, sure. Are you feeling queasy?' He slipped off his shoe and handed over his sock.

'Nope,' said Flunk who picked up his brother, popped him up in the sock and zipped it shut. 'Like I said, I got some thinking to do and I need some peace and quiet.'

He wasn't about to let go of the atomic liquidizer though. Flunk needed to do a bit more thinking.

Just then a voice shouted out from the 4D hologram phone. 'Flunk, Zultar, one of you pick up, it's your father.'

Flunk didn't really want to talk to his dad because he was trying to think but he knew he'd get told off later if he didn't accept the call. He pressed a button and his dad's hologram appeared in the room. 'Your mother's a bit busy,' he said. 'I've tied her to a chair and told her that if she interrupts she'll be making her own tea for the rest of her life. I've come to a decision. I'm completely fed up with every other alien in the galaxy despising us. I've got no friends at all. So, those humans in the cargo bay – take them home. They're not the solution to the power problem on Nrrmmff. We'll just have to find something else.'

'Daddy, I was going to say all that! Maybe not with

all those big words but you just said everything what I wanted to say! I figured it out like you.'

'Good boy,' said his dad.

'And, er, Daddy,' said Flunk. 'I've another idea.'

'It's not that one about putting custard on a sandwich again, is it?' asked his dad. 'Because I've told you before, it won't work, son. Too runny.'

'It's not about sandwiches, Dad, no. I think I know how to solve our power problem. It's me! I can do it! I had a go on one of those runny around wheels and I'm brilliant at it! I think I could power Nrrmmff on my own . . . for years!'

'Wonderful,' said his dad. 'Where's your brother,

by the way?'

'Er, he just popped to the bathroom,' said Flunk, quickly hiding the Sick Sock in a desk drawer. Flunk decided he'd let him out only after they'd arrived back on Nrrmmff.

After a quick cup of iced coffee, the Fish Fingers made Flunk promise not to reveal their secret identities. The new ship's captain happily agreed. Then he ordered the Nrrmmffian troops to release the athletes who were very understanding about the whole thing. In fact, they went around shaking hands with all the Nrrmmffians, saying, 'No hard feelings because it must be very difficult when your entire planet's about to be wiped out.'

HOME SWEET HOME

When the spaceship returned to Earth, it touched down at Tumchester Stadium. The crowds had long since gone home and the only people to greet it were agents from the M25 who'd managed to track the spaceship on their interstellar radar.

Flunk shook hands with Agent Lemon. 'This time we really, really, really do come in peace,' he said. 'Cross my hearts. I've got seven of them, you know.'

'That's very interesting,' said Agent Lemon, whose life's ambition had always been to have an alien friend.

As Ricky Zigzag was coming down the ramp he spotted Gary, Bel, Ruby and Morris. 'Hey, kiddos, wait up!' he shouted, rushing over and giving them all hugs. 'I didn't know you guys were on board! How did that happen?'

'Er, we just kind of got mixed up in the crowd,' fibbed Gary.

'The Nrrmmffians locked us in a laundry cupboard,' added Bel. 'That's probably why we didn't bump into you before. I think they forgot about us until now.'

'Oh, I didn't realise,' said Ricky. 'I hope you didn't get too upset. By the way, have you seen some superhero dudes? I think they're called the Fish Fingers or something.'

'Can't say we have,' said Morris.

'Well, let me tell you, those guys are superstars,' said Ricky. 'Somehow they saved everybody and if I ever get the chance to ask them for their autographs, now that would be amazing.'

The children blushed, then smiled, then giggled until their sides hurt.

A decision was made to postpone the Trophy Games, but at Fish Street School a few days later they held a special hurdles race in honour of Ricky Zigzag. The superstar himself was there as guest of honour and it was a very grand affair indeed. Hundreds of parents crowded onto the school field to watch. First there were heats and semi-finals and this whittled the athletes down to the six fastest in the school. The hot favourite was Snoddy, who looked very impressive in the early rounds. Ruby and Gary both made it through to the final too and some of the spectators thought they may have been saving some of their energy for the last race. In the crowd, Ruby's gran chatted merrily to Gary's dad, Bel's parents handed round freshly cooked samosas and even Morris's mum turned up. (Luckily she hadn't brought any of her home cooking since it only came in one colour – black – and one flavour – burnt.) Snoddy's dad came with his dog, Belcher, and before the start of the big race the two of them paraded around the running track even though there was a sign up which read 'No dog walking allowed'. Everyone was a bit too scared to tell them off though.

The headteacher Mrs Pompidoor announced that the grand final would start in a few minutes and all the runners went to line up. Snoddy was on the outside lane closest to the crowd. Ruby was on his right and Gary was next to her.

As the spectators settled down, Snoddy said to Ruby, 'Careful not to trip over any gnomes. I'd hate to see you fall flat on your face again.'

Ruby ignored him but Gary said, 'Right salad, wrong cucumber.' It was something Agent Lemon had said and at the time Gary had thought it was very confusing. He hoped it would mess with Snoddy's brain and it did.

'Eh? You what?' said Snoddy.

Gary then hit him with words of wisdom he'd got from Ruby's gran (via Ruby). 'You know, Ruby's not as green as she is cabbage-looking. She runs like the clappers.'

Snoddy's mind went blank. And as he stood puzzling over what nonsense Gary had said, the race gun went off and it took him completely by surprise.

At the first hurdle Ruby was in front with Gary on her shoulder followed by the other three racers and Snoddy bringing up the rear. But Snoddy was furious. He knew he'd been tricked and his anger spurred him on. Hurdle by hurdle he caught up. By the halfway point he was neck and neck with Gary (who was still clinging on to second) and they were both closing in on Ruby. She glanced over her shoulder and smiled. She knew she had an extra gear and she shifted into it now. She glided smoothly over the next hurdle and opened up a good lead. Snoddy realised he'd never catch her but at least he could finish second. The rest of the pack was far behind and he only had to beat Gary, just like he always did. Snoddy kicked again, rising high over the next hurdle and landing in front of his rival but as he did so, his legs did the splits as he slipped on a huge pile of doggy doo left by his own grizzly mutt, Belcher. Snoddy lay on the floor, wiping the mess off his trainers and scraping his mucky fingers on the grass as all the other runners skipped past him.

'That'll teach your dad to read the signs properly,

Snoddy!' shouted a voice from the crowd that sounded a lot like Morris's.

Ruby had a wonderful moment of triumph as she coasted through the tape that spanned the winning line. She was easily ten yards in front of the next runner, who was Gary. The crowd gave a huge cheer and Ruby got a big hug from her gran and her idol (everybody's idol) Ricky Zigzag.

After the race, Ricky invited all of the Fish Fingers to tea and he even let them choose the restaurant. They picked their favourite fast food place, Big Momma's, which had recently reopened after refurbishment. As they gazed at the menu, the children thought about ordering chicken nuggets but they all opted for burgers instead. After everything they'd been through it seemed like the most sensible option. They sat for a long time eating, drinking and listening to Ricky tell them all about the races he'd won and the places he'd been. 'Doesn't matter where I go though,' he said, 'Tumchester is home and it always will be.'

The Fish Fingers nodded. They couldn't agree more.

Just then a girl in a Big Momma uniform walked past, carrying a tray of french fries and chicken nuggets. 'Did you guys order these?' she asked.

'No, not us,' said Morris looking at the tray. As the waitress went off to find the food's rightful owner though, Morris did a double take. He wasn't sure but for a split second he thought he saw one of the nuggets wink its eye and adjust the button on its very tight trousers.

ACKNOWLEDGEMENTS

You may think I use this bit in the book to say hello to all those people I care about but forgot to send Christmas cards to. Nothing could be further from the truth. However while I am here, I would quickly like to say thank you to my Aunty Margaret for the Christmas jumper because it looks great on me. Where was I? Oh yes, this section is all about thanking those people who have worked tirelessly to help bring my third book into the world.

Liz Bankes, Roger & Ann Beresford, Rhona Langan, Euan Smith, Mark Cameron, Kev, Sue, Karl & Jodie McCarthy, Lara & James Routh, Estela & Lilia Green, Richard & Wendy Askam, Dave, Louisa, Kitty & Jack Williams, Rebecca Kelly, Mark Barnsley, Tony & Suzanne Sharkey, Mike Ward, Kathryn Ross, Alex Hardy, Jon, Jacqui, Edris & Jake Doyle, Richard, Becky, Tilly & Dougie Marsden, Andrew Rowley, Jessica Kenmore, Rory O'Connor & Fauzia Khan, Rufus & Silas Khan O'Connor, Clare Burkhill-Howarth, John & Margaret Merrick, Shane, Louisa, Niamh, Grace & Erin Merrick, Alfie Hosker, Lynne Allison & Brooke Allison, Jim Askam, Mark & Gabby Nickson, Noel, Fergal & Niamh Curry, Robert

Baldock, Anne Perry, Geoff Foster, Ian Moore, Bill & Amanda Finch, Mark Jones, Chris Twigger, Paul Gilbert, Ian Young, Brendon & Leah Guildford, Chris & Angela Pinckard, Bill & Henry Haw, Rachel McLaren, Marvyn Dickinson, Kerry Allison, Phil Crabb, Sonny, Dawn, Storm & Sonny-Jay Hanley, Nigel Green, Toshiko Ishizaki, Mark Robinson, Richard, Fran & Jamie Hannan, Rachel Chadwick, Barney & Molly Porter, Sarah Hunt, Danny Howarth, James MacMillan, Dorota Mokszanska, Julie Colley, Wilbert Walsh, Jim, Sam & Sean Brassil, Linda Bailey, Rebecca Thackrah, Jo Wragg, Deborah Harrison, Anne Hargrave, Christine Wood, Kathy Heeley, Jane Hollick, Sarah Werkman, Sean Mohan, Nela Willis, Kim Lindsay, Dot Staunton & Merlin & Dylan Owen, Helen Spencer & Steve Drayton, John Clayton, Sian Williams & Paul Woolwich, Seth & Eve Woolwich-Williams, Sunita Shroff, Shalimar Poulin, Aunty Gladys, Richard, Ellen, Ashley, Chris & Gemma Beresford, Andy, Roz, Josh & Izzy Beresford. And all the staff & pupils of Highfield Primary School in Leeds.

A very massive thank you to Vicky Barker (illustrator extraordinaire) and as always the most massivest thanks in the universe go to my two brilliant daughters Hayley & Laura.

FIND OUT HOW IT ALL BEGAN FOR GARY, BEL, RUBY AND MORRIS IN THEIR FIRST ADVENTURE . . .

After a magical, crisp-loving elf turns them into superheroes, **The Chimp**, **Nightingale**, **KangaRuby** and **Slug Boy** must rescue Tumchester from a pair of super-scary and super-hairy villains. But first the **Fabulous Four Fish Fingers** must learn to work as a team (and remember not to step on Slug Boy).

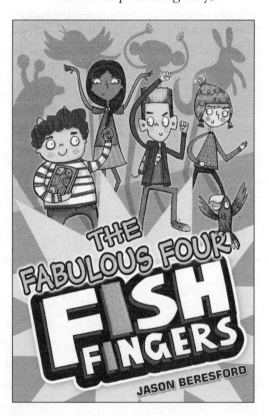

WARNING!!!!! This book contains a panteater. He will steal your sweets. And eat your pants.

The gang are thrilled to win a school trip to Transyldovia. But amid all the skiing and snow-filled fun, something strange is afoot. It starts with a runway toilet and rapidly snowballs into a wild and dangerous adventure . . .

Flying pigs . . . Vampires . . . BEETROOT!!!

Will the Fish Fingers Survive?

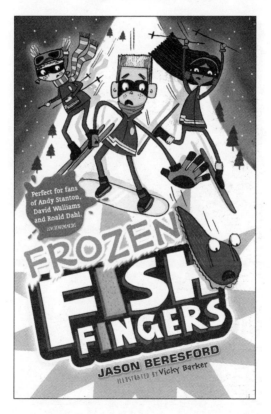

Perfect for fans of Andy Stanton, David Walliams and Roald Dahl.
LOVEREADING4KIDS

FROZEN FISH FINGERS

JASON BERESFORD

ILLUSTRATED BY Vicky Barker

Get ready for a crazy adventure . . .

IF YOU HAD A MAGIC QUILL PEN that MADE ALL YOUR DRAWINGS REAL . . . WHAt WOULD YOU DRAW?

MORE FUNNY FICTION FROM CATNIP

TWO FRIENDS AND A MAGIC FEATHER... WHAT COULD POSSIBLY GO WRONG?

'Funny with a capital F' Mo O'Hara

JACK DASH
AND THE
MAGIC FEATHER

By
SOPHIE PLOWDEN

Illustrated by
Judy Brown

When Jack Dash finds the magic feather, things go from DULL to AWESOME in 0.6 seconds. He can have anything he wants!

Only it turns out Jack isn't very good at drawing . . . and his life is soon full of unexpected chaos, frilly knickers and a sea lion.

When he finds himself on the run, it's time for Jack to save the day. Can he be quick on the draw??